MASTER OF PEMBERLEY

A Pride and Prejudice Variation

Jane Grix

Cover design by beetifulbookcovers.com
Formatting by Polgarus Studio

To learn about new books and short stories by Jane Grix, sign up for her mailing list at: www.janegrix.com

CHAPTER ONE

Fitzwilliam Darcy knew that it was his duty to remarry, although he did not look forward to the process. He invited his cousin Colonel Fitzwilliam to dine at his house in London to discuss strategies. He waited until the meal was finished and they were drinking port in front of a fireplace to broach the subject. "It is time I married again. Do you have any suggestions?"

The Colonel looked at him with surprise. "What – already? Has it been a year?"

"A year and two days."

"I hadn't realized it had been so long since Anne died."

"No, neither had I until my valet asked me this morning which waistcoat I wished to wear." Darcy smiled grimly. "It feels strange to be wearing a colour other than black."

"If you don't wish to abandon your mourning, don't."

Darcy shook his head. "My grief, my mourning, is a private matter and completely unrelated to my choice of attire. I will meet society's expectations, but I will not draw undue attention to myself by continuing to wear black."

The Colonel glanced over at him. "That's a shame. Black looks good on you. Very imposing."

"Is that why you joined the regiment, because you look good in red?"

The Colonel grinned. "Don't tell the Earl."

Darcy sipped his drink, and then returned to the task at hand. "I suppose I could wait until the Season starts in the spring to find a wife, but I would prefer to avoid that madhouse."

"You just don't want to dance."

Darcy didn't comment. He and his cousins had shared dancing instructors when they were younger. He could perform the steps but felt that the activity was generally ridiculous and a waste of time. If he wished to exercise, he would walk or ride. If he wished to converse, he would sit and have a rational conversation. It was impossible to engage in conversation in a crowd with loud music, unable to speak two sentences together without being separated by the variations of the dance movements.

"You are much more aware of potential candidates than I," Darcy said. "Do you have any suggestions?"

The Colonel said, "Not unless you are looking for a wealthy widow." As a second son, he would have to marry money if he wished to live at the level he had been born to.

"No, I would prefer a younger woman, not a woman set in her ways."

"Will a young woman be capable of running Pemberley?"

"She will learn."

"What if she doesn't?"

He frowned. "I will make certain that the woman I marry is intelligent."

"You won't be swayed by a pleasing figure and captivating smile?"

"Naturally, I would prefer to wed an attractive woman, but she does not have to be a diamond of the first water." He thought for a moment. "I would like her to be taller than Anne, though." And sturdier, he mentally added but considered it too indelicate to say aloud.

His first wife, the former Anne de Bourgh, had been small and frail. She had never complained, but he had always been concerned, being careful not to crush her the few times they had been intimate.

"With nice wide, child-bearing hips?"

Darcy smiled ruefully. It appeared that his cousin could read his thoughts. They both knew that Pemberley needed a male heir – several if possible. He had two younger brothers who had died – one shortly after birth and the second from a childhood accident at age seven. Ideally he would like to have two or three sons to secure an orderly transition of ownership when he died. He did not want Pemberley to fall into the hands of his distant cousin Julian Darcy. He said lightly, "Exactly how does one go about discerning the width of a woman's hips? With the current fashions, it is almost impossible to discover if a woman has a proper waist."

"Take a dressmaker's tape to Almacks. I am certain that none of the matchmaking mothers will mind if you take measurements."

Darcy raised one eyebrow at his cousin's absurdity.

The Colonel persisted. "They would never refuse a request from a man with your income. I believe they would line up their daughters without a stitch on if they thought it would result in a marriage proposal." He laughed at his own humour.

"You have a vulgar mind."

"No, I am just not a monk like you."

Darcy knew this was a reference to a conversation they'd had a week earlier. Darcy had declined his cousin's invitation to go to a brothel while he was in town. The Colonel had said, "I understand and respect your not wanting to go when Anne was alive, but what is holding you back now? She is dead. And it is not as if I am asking you to pick up a harlot on some back street. Madame Lucienne's establishment is very clean, very discrete, very respectable."

His cousin could not see the irony in describing a whorehouse as respectable, but as the second son of an Earl, he had been reared in a more worldly environment. Many gentlemen of the *haut ton* thought nothing of keeping a mistress or frequenting a brothel.

Darcy had been unable to explain to him his moral objections to prostitution, so he had ended the conversation by saying that he did not want to expose himself to disease.

They were both silent for a few minutes, then the Colonel asked, "Do you still miss her?"

That was difficult to answer. His cousin Anne had always been a part of his life. Darcy had known since he was a child that they were destined to marry. In some ways he cared for her as he cared for his younger sister Georgiana or his cousin the Colonel.

Anne was part of his family and it had been his duty to protect her. When they were of a proper age and her doctors thought her well enough to marry, they married. Neither of them were of a disposition to experience or desire *une grande passion*, but they treated each other with mutual respect, and their marriage had been a happy one.

A year later Juliette was born.

Darcy thought of his daughter. She was a bright, beautiful child, and fortunately much stronger than Anne had ever been. He was sorry that Anne had not lived to be able to see her grow into a young woman.

"Yes, I miss Anne," he said finally. "But I would not wish her back again. She was ill for so long, I believe her death was a blessed release."

The Colonel nodded. "I miss her, too."

* * *

A few days later, Darcy met his friend Charles Bingley at a dinner at the home of another friend. Bingley invited him to go to Hertfordshire. He had recently rented a house there, and he wanted to show it off. "Come down and spend a few weeks."

"Who else will be there?"

"Just my two sisters and Mr. Hurst."

At first Darcy thought he would decline. If he was

going to spend time in the country, he would prefer to be at Pemberley with Georgiana and Juliette. But then he remembered that one of Bingley's sisters was unmarried. Miss Caroline Bingley was a tall, handsome woman with a respectable fortune of twenty thousand pounds. She had been reasonably educated at a private seminary in town. She was not as studious as Anne had been, but then few women were. He tried to remember any of their conversations. She seemed like a well-bred young woman, not silly or giddy. He could not remember if she played the pianoforte, or if that had been her older, married sister. He seemed to remember that she spoke French and some Italian. She wasn't timid or shy. Anne had been painfully shy and had only been comfortable conversing with members of her family.

Miss Bingley had visited Pemberley once before Anne died. She had played briefly with Juliette and was kind to Georgiana.

He considered her now as a potential wife for himself and as a stepmother for his daughter. One thing in her favour was that her parents were not alive. Lady Catherine de Bourgh was his mother-in-law and she was more than sufficient. He did not want another. The second thing in her favour was that Charles Bingley was her brother.

He'd met Bingley a few years earlier at Tattersalls. They had both been looking to purchase a horse. Darcy had been impressed with Bingley's easy manners, his openness and the docility of his temper. Since then, they had maintained a steady friendship. It would be good to have Bingley as a brother by marriage.

Bingley's fortune, more than one hundred thousand pounds, had been acquired by trade two generations back, but as far as Darcy knew, he had no embarrassing close connections.

Darcy did not consider himself a snob. Although his grandfather was an Earl, he did not need to marry into the aristocracy. Additionally, he thought that just as in horse breeding, he might be able to produce healthier offspring if he added some common stock to the mix. Living with Anne and watching her suffer had made him rethink the wisdom of having cousins marry.

"Yes, I will come," Darcy said.

He would go to Hertfordshire and determine whether he wanted to marry Caroline Bingley. That would be much easier than trying to find a suitable woman in London. Most people were on their best behaviour when in society, and there was insufficient time and opportunity to get to know anyone deeply. But at a house party, over the course of a month or two, he would be able to observe Miss Bingley on a daily basis in more natural, unguarded moments and ultimately make a reasoned decision.

"Excellent," Bingley said. "You can meet all my new neighbours. There is a ball in three days."

For a moment Darcy regretted his acceptance. But he could not back out now, even if there would be dancing.

* * *

Darcy looked around the Meryton Assembly room. He did not want to be there, but in politeness to his host, he could not decline. He watched as Bingley became acquainted with all the principal people in the room. He danced every dance. Darcy was amazed by his cheerful fortitude. Bingley was like his favourite hunter dog, eager and friendly.

Although Mr. Darcy disliked dancing, he knew that most women liked it, and Mr. Bingley's sisters would be offended if he did not dance with them, so he dutifully danced one dance with Mrs. Hurst and one with Miss Bingley. Several people sought an introduction with him, but he ignored them.

Assemblies such as this were to be endured rather

than enjoyed.

He stood to one side of the room, wondering how soon the evening would end. He opened the gold watch on the end of his fob, glanced at it briefly, and then shut the case closed.

Bingley came from the dance for a few minutes to accost him.

"Come, Darcy," he said. "I must have you dance. I hate to see you standing about by yourself in this stupid manner. You had much better dance."

Darcy began to think it might have been a mistake to come to Hertfordshire, if Bingley was going to insist that he interact with all his low born neighbours. He was glad he had brought his own carriage so he could leave quickly if the visit became tedious.

And why did everyone want him to dance? Sometimes it felt like a conspiracy. "I certainly shall not. You know how I detest it, unless I am particularly acquainted with my partner. Your sisters are engaged, and there is not another woman in the room, whom it would not be a punishment to me to stand up with."

Bingley laughed. "I would not be so fastidious as you are for a kingdom! Upon my honour, I never met with so many pleasant girls in my life as I have this evening. Several of them are uncommonly pretty."

Bingley was easy to please. Darcy looked around the room. He saw Bingley's partner. He believed her last name was Bennet. She was slim and fair-haired. "You are dancing with the only handsome girl in the room."

"Oh! She is the most beautiful creature I ever beheld. But there is one of her sisters sitting down just behind you, who is very pretty, and I dare say, very agreeable. Do let me ask my partner to introduce you."

Darcy asked, "Whom do you mean?" and turning around, he looked for a moment at the eldest Miss Bennet. She was of average height with dark hair and dark eyes that met his gaze briefly. He looked away and said in a lower tone to Bingley, "She is tolerable; but not handsome enough to tempt me; and I am in no humour at present to give consequence to young ladies who are slighted by other men."

"You are a fool, Darcy," Bingley said.

"You had better return to your partner and enjoy her smiles, for you are wasting your time with me."

Bingley followed his advice. Darcy walked to the other side of the room and served himself a cup of punch. As he sipped the disgustingly sweet liquid, he surveyed the room. He saw the eldest Bennet girl again, this time talking with two other young women. With detachment, he saw that her figure was light and pleasing with a fuller bosom than her sister's. The flickering candlelight illuminated her face and neck. She was talking in an animated manner, laughing, which gave her face added beauty. As if with one motion the two young women speaking to her looked over at him, blushed when they saw he was watching them, and then looked quickly away.

They both laughed nervously as if they had been caught talking about him.

They said something to Miss Bennet, and she turned to look at him herself. She observed him coolly with the poise of a woman many years her senior.

She had dark, arresting eyes.

For a second or two they stared at each other across the room, and then she calmly turned back to her friends, seemingly unconcerned.

Darcy stiffened. He felt as if he had been judged and found wanting.

He feared that she must have overheard what he said earlier, and he regretted his rash words. Not the sentiment behind them, but that she had overheard and been insulted.

He prided himself on his correct manners, but to

apologize would only strengthen the offense, so he would say nothing and hope that she would forget the matter completely. He did not like to be rude, but sometimes it was inevitable.

He let his breath out slowly, striving to regain his natural equilibrium. This was yet another reason why he disliked large public gatherings. Whenever a hundred people were in a room, there were bound to be misunderstandings, offense and drama.

He much preferred the peace and order of Pemberley.

* * *

When the Bennet family returned home, they found Mr. Bennet still up. He had been reading but set aside the volume as they entered the sitting room. Mrs. Bennet spoke as she entered the room. "Oh, Mr. Bennet, it was a most excellent ball. I wish you could have been there and seen Jane's triumph. Mr. Bingley danced with her twice." She chatted on, describing the evening in the greatest detail: who danced with whom and what the major attendees had been wearing.

After twenty-three years of marriage, Mr. Bennet knew he did not need to pay much attention to his wife. She was happy to talk as long as he periodically nodded or smiled. Eventually she declared that she was too exhausted to talk any longer and she must get to bed. "But I shall sleep well knowing that Mr. Bingley found Jane to be the prettiest girl in the room. He said as much to Mr. Robinson and Charlotte Lucas overheard him." She sighed. "It gives me hope, Mr. Bennet."

Mr. Bennet did not have to ask what her hopes were, for she had talked of little else since Mr. Bingley had moved into the neighbourhood, renting a large manor house – Netherfield Park. Mrs. Bennet hoped that Mr. Bingley who was rumoured to have a fortunate of five thousand pounds a year would fall in love and marry one of their five daughters.

Mr. Bennet turned to his oldest daughter, Elizabeth. "And you, Lizzy? Did you have a pleasant evening?'

Elizabeth nodded. "Yes, sir. Very enjoyable. But then, I love to dance."

Lydia interrupted their conversation by announcing, "Kitty and I danced every dance and Mary only danced twice."

Mrs. Bennet said, "Mary needs to smile more and stand up straight." She turned to her middle daughter. "I believe you have been sitting too long at the pianoforte, hunching your shoulders. You'll never get a husband if you ruin your posture."

"Perhaps I don't wish to get a husband," Mary said quietly.

"Not get a husband?" Mrs. Bennet gasped. "For all your book reading, your head is filled with nonsense. Mr. Bennet, I demand that you speak to your daughter."

"Good night," he said firmly and guided them both towards the door. "It is too late to discuss the matter fully. Go to bed, everyone. Good night, Mrs. Bennet."

She wished to prolong the discussion, but the determined look on his face deterred her, so they all left the sitting room and headed upstairs.

"Lizzy," Mrs. Bennet said as they paused outside her bedroom door. "Try not to fret about Mr. Darcy and the dreadful things he said this evening."

Elizabeth startled. She hadn't given him much thought at all, other than to laugh at his rudeness with her friends. "Don't worry. I won't lose any sleep over it."

Mrs. Bennet continued. "I am glad. It must have been mortifying to hear that you were not handsome enough to dance with." She patted her arm. "You may not be as beautiful as Jane, but you are a pretty girl, in your own way."

Elizabeth smiled, not taking offense. In looks she took after her own mother, who had died in childbirth. When she was a baby her father had married again, so Mrs. Bennet was her stepmother. Mrs. Bennet had been a beauty in her youth and was still a handsome woman with fair hair and blue eyes.

"And you don't lose a thing by not suiting his fancy, even if he does have ten thousand pounds a year. For he is a most disagreeable, horrid man, not at all worth pleasing. So high and mighty. Did you notice the way he walked here and there, fancying himself so very great?"

He did seem to be arrogant, dismissive of nearly everyone in the room. "No. I was more pleasantly occupied, enjoying the evening."

"I'm glad. But what a scowl he has – looking down on all of us."

Elizabeth smiled. She said, "With his height, by necessity, he must look down on almost everyone."

Mrs. Bennet did not acknowledge her attempt at humour. Instead she hid a yawn behind her hand and said, "Not handsome enough to dance with. Try not to think about it."

She would not, if her stepmother would not keep reminding her. "I will try. Good night, ma'am."

"Good night, Lizzy." She continued down the

hall. "Kitty," she said loudly, "Make certain you wash your face. I noticed a spot on your chin tonight."

Elizabeth entered her bedroom that she shared with her sister Jane and closed the door. "At last we can talk. Tell me about Mr. Bingley."

Jane smiled and blushed, which told Elizabeth exactly what she wanted to know.

Jane turned her back so Elizabeth could unfasten her ball gown. "I like him," Jane said. "He is just what a young man ought to be: sensible, good humoured, lively; and I never saw such happy manners – so much ease with such perfect good breeding."

And so different from his tall, disagreeable friend. Elizabeth said, "He's handsome, too, which is always an advantage."

"I believe I would like him even if he weren't handsome."

"I believe you would. But then, I don't think you've ever met anyone you haven't liked." Jane thought everyone in the world was good and kind. Elizabeth, only two years older, knew differently.

Jane said, "That is not what I meant."

Elizabeth frowned. "Don't tell me you have fallen in love with him at first sight."

She turned her back so that Jane could undo her

dress as well.

"No, of course not," Jane said quickly. "That would be silly. I am not like Lydia."

"Thank goodness." At fifteen, Lydia fancied herself in love every week with a different gentleman.

They slipped out of their clothes, folded them neatly and changed into their nightgowns. Elizabeth sat before a mirror so she could remove the ribbons and hairpins from her ornate hairstyle. She ran her fingers through her hair, massaging her scalp, then brushed her hair and braided it so it wouldn't tangle during the night. It was a trial to have naturally curly hair. Her sisters had to use curling tongs or sleep with papers to make their hair curl, but she had to keep hers under control or she would look unkempt.

"Did you have a nice evening?" Jane asked once they were both settled in the bed that they shared.

"Yes, I did."

"I'm sorry Mr. Bingley's friend was unkind, but he probably did not mean to be overheard."

To Elizabeth, it seemed as if everyone was taking his comment more seriously than she had. "If Mr. Darcy does not wish to be overheard, he should not speak."

"Miss Bingley says that he does not speak much unless among his intimate acquaintances."

Mr. Bingley's sister was a fine lady, expensively attired, who appeared to be almost as proud as Mr. Darcy. She had looked at everyone with a superior sneer. Elizabeth said, "Considering his manners, it is a wonder that any of Mr. Darcy's acquaintances would wish to be intimate."

"Miss Bingley said he is remarkably agreeable."

"Then Miss Bingley and I have different definitions of the word."

"Remember, he is a widower," Jane added gently.

"Does that give him permission to be rude?"

"No, but perhaps the ball brought back memories of his wife and made him sad."

Elizabeth sighed. "You are too tender-hearted. I am sorry for anyone who has lost his life's companion, but if he is still too broken-hearted to be civil, he should stay home."

"Did his comments upset you?"

"A little," Elizabeth admitted. "But nothing to signify." As she turned on her side and adjusted her pillow, she idly wondered what the party at Netherfield thought of the evening.

CHAPTER TWO

That evening Mr. Bingley and his party sat in one of Netherfield's elegantly furnished sitting rooms. Mr. Bingley said, "I have never met with pleasanter people or prettier girls in my life."

Mr. Darcy said, "Truly?" He knew that Bingley was easily pleased, but for himself, he had only seen a collection of people in whom there was little beauty and no fashion. He did not feel the smallest interest in furthering an acquaintance with any of them. "I grant you, Miss Jane Bennet is a pretty girl," he said finally.

"Pretty?" Bingley scoffed. "You must be blind. She is the most beautiful creature."

Darcy frowned. He had seen Bingley in love before, but he had rarely been so effusive. "Beauty is as beauty does."

"She is as beautiful inside as she is outside."

"And how could you possibly know that after five minutes conversation?"

"Possibly twenty," Bingley said, smiling wryly. "I'll admit, I don't know her completely yet, but I look forward to getting to know her better."

"I agree," Miss Bingley said. "She seems like a sweet girl."

Darcy spoke to her. "Did you enjoy the evening, Miss Bingley?"

She smiled. "Yes. I knew that the society would not be as refined as what I am accustomed to in town, so I did not expect much. But it was a pleasant evening, overall. I enjoyed dancing and the musicians made only a few mistakes."

He appreciated her sanguine attitude.

Miss Bingley said, "And you, sir. How did you like the evening?"

He hadn't, but there was no point in dwelling on the negative. "Well enough. But I am glad to be back at Netherfield. You have a good house here, Bingley. It is very comfortable."

"It is nothing compared to Pemberley."

Miss Bingley said, "I believe Pemberley is one of the most beautiful homes I've ever seen. Such a happy combination of taste and elegance. I thoroughly enjoyed my visit there."

And perhaps one day she would be its mistress. "Thank you."

Over the next two weeks, they attended several dinners in the neighbourhood. Darcy watched Caroline Bingley as she interacted with society that was beneath her own. She was always elegantly dressed and she was an excellent card player. He found her manners reserved but not haughty. She knew what to say and what not to say. If she found a situation awkward or in poor taste, she usually waited until the evening had ended before commenting on the matter privately at home. He thought that with proper training, she would be able to direct the household staff at Pemberley.

All he had to decide now was whether he wanted her in his bed as well as mother to his future children.

Procreation was a simple matter of biology. Theoretically any willing, reasonably attractive woman would do. Caroline Bingley was attractive and appeared to enjoy his attentions.

But would she be a good model for their children?

One of the evenings they were already seated in a sitting room at Lucas Lodge when the Bennet family arrived. Mr. Bennet was a conservatively dressed, quiet gentleman; his wife was overdressed, overly talkative and vulgar. Darcy watched with disgust as she fawned over Bingley, but his friend treated her with patience. He was surprised to learn that they had five daughters, all of whom who were in attendance, even the youngest two, who appeared quite young to be in company. They were silly, giggly girls.

Upon further observation, he discovered that Miss Jane Bennet was a pleasant young woman with a calm, even temper. She seemed to enjoy Bingley's attentions, but was not overly affected by them. He was glad to see that she was not actively encouraging him. Bingley could do much better for himself.

He noticed the eldest Miss Bennet as well. Her name was Elizabeth, sometimes called Eliza or even Lizzy by her acquaintances. In his opinion Lizzy was an unattractive appellation more suited to a child than a grown woman. At first he had dismissed her as hardly having any beauty, but in observing her in conversation with others, he saw that her dark eyes brimmed with intelligence. And her manners, although not of those of the fashionable world, had an easy playfulness that was surprisingly attractive.

He found himself drawn to her, intrigued by what she might be saying, so he made an effort to overhear her conversations with others. He listened as she spoke to Colonel Forster, the commanding officer of the local regiment. She teased that gentleman to give another ball at Meryton. Later, when she was sitting down, he walked past and she said, "Mr. Darcy."

He paused.

She smiled and turned to look up at him. "Did you not think that I expressed myself uncommonly well just now?"

He checked himself. He did not think she had noticed his attention. To reduce any false hopes she might be harbouring, he said coolly, "Yes, dancing is a subject which always makes a lady energetic."

"And you find amusement in that."

Her tone challenged him. "Not particularly, it is just that I do not find the exercise as appealing as most everyone else does. I avoid it whenever possible."

"Then I feel sorry for you, because I find dancing to be one of life's greatest pleasures."

The smile in her eyes was entrancing and for a moment he could think of nothing to say.

Miss Lucas approached them and said, "Excuse me, sir, but I must take Miss Bennet away. Come, Eliza, you promised to play and sing a song for us."

Darcy was relieved, grateful for the respite. He did not want to be attracted to Miss Bennet, even fleetingly.

He watched with calm observation as she played.

Her performance was pleasing, though by no means capital. She had a naturally pretty voice, but it had not been classically trained. After two songs, and before she could reply to the entreaties of several that she would sing again, her sister Mary volunteered to play, almost pushing Miss Bennet aside. She played the pianoforte twice as well as her older sister, but she had a pedantic air and conceited manner that irritated him, lessening his enjoyment. The younger Miss Bennets requested that she play some Scotch and Irish airs so they could dance.

Darcy watched in annoyance as several of the Lucases and some officers joined them in dancing. With all the noise and movement, there would be no more conversation tonight. He walked over to join Bingley, but before he reached him, that gentleman took Miss Jane Bennet by the hand and walked with her to the makeshift dance floor.

Darcy stood back, out of the way, wondering how soon they would be able to leave to return to Netherfield. He opened his fob watch briefly, then snapped it shut.

Sir William Lucas approached. He was a simple, rotund man who had been in trade and elevated to the Knighthood. He said cheerfully, "Do you intend to join them in the dance, sir?"

Darcy meant to decline, but at that moment Elizabeth Bennet moved towards them and Sir William said, "And here is a partner for you – Miss Eliza. Mr. Darcy, you cannot refuse to dance, I am sure, when so much beauty is before you."

Elizabeth's face flamed with embarrassment and for a few seconds her eyes met his, then looked away. "Forgive me, sir," she said quickly to Sir William, "I have not the least intention of dancing. I entreat you not to suppose that I moved this way in order to beg for a partner."

Darcy, appalled by the social awkwardness of the situation, tried to make amends. "I would appreciate it, if you would do me the honour." It was the civil thing to do. He held out his hand.

"No, thank you."

Darcy was stunned. It was the first time he had ever been rejected.

Sir William persisted. "Miss Eliza, you are an excellent dancer. Please do not deprive everyone in the room the joy of watching you dance."

Darcy added his own persuasion. "And perhaps you could teach me the pleasure of dancing."

She looked at him coolly. "You are all politeness, sir, but I fear that task is beyond me." She bowed her head slightly and walked on, away from them. Sir

William left to pester someone else.

He stood as if set in stone, not knowing whether to be stung or relieved by her refusal.

Miss Bingley approached him. "I can guess the subject of your reverie," she said in a low tone.

"I should imagine not."

"You are considering how insupportable it would be to pass many evenings in this manner – in such insipid society."

She was remarkably perceptive. Those had been his exact feelings only a few minutes before. "No, my mind is more agreeably engaged."

"On what, may I ask?"

"I have been meditating on the very great pleasure which a pair of fine eyes in the face of a pretty woman can bestow."

Miss Bingley dropped her eyelashes and looked up at him through them in a flirtatious manner. "Dare I ask whose eyes have inspired such reflections?"

He could not lie. "Miss Bennet."

"Miss Elizabeth Bennet?" repeated Miss Bingley. "I am all astonishment. How long has she been such a favourite?"

Darcy wished he had kept his thoughts to himself. "She is not a favourite," he said clearly. "She has pretty eyes, that is all."

"I am relieved," Miss Bingley said archly. "For a moment, I was afraid that I would have to wish you joy. Can you imagine having such a mother-in-law? She would always be visiting at Pemberley. You would never have a moment's peace with her underfoot."

Darcy said nothing. Although he knew that women's minds often jumped from admiration to love, from love to matrimony in a moment, he recognized the wisdom of her words. He did not want Mrs. Bennet as a mother-in-law. No sensible man would.

He must ignore Miss Bennet and not allow himself to be distracted by her fine eyes.

* * *

A few days later Jane was pleased to receive an invitation to dine with Miss Bingley and her sister. Mrs. Bennet snatched the letter from her hands and read it eagerly. She was annoyed to discover that the men would not be present because they were dining with the officers. "But all is not lost," she said cheerfully. "You will go on horseback."

"On horseback?" Jane said. "Can I not have the carriage?"

"Absolutely not, for I think it will rain."

"But if it rains, it would be better if I had the carriage."

"No, for it rains, you may have to spend the night."

"Mother," Elizabeth protested. "You cannot be serious."

Mrs. Bennet turned on her. "Do you want Jane to go over to Netherfield and not see Mr. Bingley?"

"No, but –"

"Shh. I know what I am doing." She turned to her oldest daughter. "Jane, wear your new gown with the cream lace. And if you're worried about the rain, you may take an umbrella."

"Yes, ma'am."

Mrs. Bennet saw Elizabeth's look of concern and said, "Don't worry. Jane will be fine."

But she wasn't fine.

Jane was caught in a downpour and spent the night at Netherfield. In the morning a servant from Netherfield brought a note at breakfast that said Jane was ill and that the doctor Mr. Jones had been called to visit her.

Mr. Bennet said to his wife, "Well, my dear, if your daughter should a have a dangerous fit of illness, if she should die, it will be a comfort to know that it was all in pursuit of Mr. Bingley, and under your orders."

Mrs. Bennet dismissed his fears. "No one dies from a little cold."

Elizabeth was anxious, however, and wished to visit her. The carriage wasn't available and she was no horse-woman, so she decided to walk.

Mrs. Bennet was appalled. "What are you thinking? Walking in all this mud? You won't be fit to be seen."

"I shall be fit to see Jane," Elizabeth said calmly.

"Do you want me to send for the horses?" her father asked.

"No, don't go to the bother." Her sisters Kitty and Lydia walked with her as far as Meryton, and she walked the rest of the way by herself for a total of three miles.

She crossed fields, climbed over stiles and jumped over puddles. By the time she reached the large house, she was a little tired and her stockings were dirty.

She was shown into the breakfast-parlour, where all but Jane were assembled.

"Miss Bennet," Mr. Bingley said quickly and rose from his chair. "Good morning. How can I help you?"

Mr. Darcy also rose, but he said nothing, only looked at her, frowning intently.

Perhaps he was noticing the dirty hem of her petticoats. Maybe she should have waited until the carriage was available, but she had not wanted the delay. Elizabeth said, "I am here to visit my sister, if I may."

"Certainly," Mr. Bingley said quickly. "I understand that she did not sleep well and is feverish. She is not well enough to leave her room."

"But she is receiving all proper care," Miss Bingley said quickly in a defensive tone.

"I thank you," Elizabeth said.

Mrs. Hurst was astonished. "Did you walk?"

"Yes."

"All the way? Three miles? By yourself?"

"Yes, ma'am."

Mrs. Hurst looked at Miss Bingley, who raised her eyebrows, but said nothing.

A servant was summoned to escort her upstairs to see Jane. As she left the room, Elizabeth overheard Miss Bingley laugh and say, "What can she be thinking — to scamper about the country because her sister has a cold?"

"She has a great affection for her sister which I find very becoming," Mr. Bingley said.

Elizabeth did not hear the rest of the conversation for the door closed behind her. She was glad she hadn't heard Mr. Darcy's reaction, then told herself she did not care what they thought. The only person that mattered was Jane.

But when she saw her sister, she was alarmed. Jane was pale and weak and could not speak without coughing. Elizabeth put her hand on her forehead and felt that it was burning with a strong fever. The doctor visited, declared she had a violent cold and promised her some draughts. She was told to stay in bed until she got the better of it.

Elizabeth stayed for luncheon with the plan of returning home before evening, but Jane did not want her to leave and begged her to stay. Elizabeth spoke to Mr. Bingley, and he cordially invited her to remain at Netherfield. A servant was sent to Longbourn to inform the family of her plans to stay and to bring back a supply of clothes.

Jane clutched Elizabeth's hand. "I am so glad," she said weakly. "Now I know I will get well."

* * *

Mr. Darcy could not believe his misfortune. Elizabeth Bennet was at Netherfield, distracting him completely. From the moment she had entered the breakfast room he could think of nothing but how becoming she was with her face brightened by the exercise, her skin glowing, a few wisps of her hair falling onto her shoulders. In that initial moment she looked so fresh, so untidy, it made him wonder how she would look upon awakening.

This thought both stirred and appalled him. He did not want to think of Elizabeth Bennet with those a dark, arresting eyes smiling at him as she rose from rumpled sheets.

It was unseemly. It was improper.

He was determined to think of something else and took a long walk after breakfast.

At dinner he saw her again and learned that Bingley had invited her to stay and attend to her sister. Fortunately for his state of mind, she had tidied herself. She was wearing a pretty light green dress with a square neckline that bared her long, graceful throat. Her lovely dark hair was restrained in a bun of some kind at the back of her neck, but there were a few tendrils that curled above her ears. It made him wonder if her hair was naturally curly. If he pulled a few strands outward and let go, would they bounce back like a spring?

But he would not think of that.

The dinner conversation was dull, for after asking about Jane Bennet's health, there was nothing else to say. Miss Bingley and Mrs. Hurst said several times how grieved they were, how shocking it was to have a bad cold and how excessively they disliked being ill themselves.

After dinner Elizabeth left them to go directly to her sister.

Miss Bingley waited until she had left to say, "Poor Miss Bennet. I feel sympathy for her sister Jane, but I feel more for her. She has almost no conversation."

"She is concerned about her sister," Bingley said.

"And she has no style, no taste, and no beauty."

Darcy was surprised by her sharp tone, but said nothing. Miss Bingley was free to have an opinion, naturally, but he wished she had expressed it more charitably.

Mrs. Hurst agreed. "I shall never forget her appearance this morning. She looked almost wild."

Miss Bingley added, "Her hair tonight looks as if she put it up herself."

Darcy asked pointedly, "Did you or Mrs. Hurst offer her the services of your lady's maid?"

Miss Bingley's eyes widened at his implied barb, and she hastened to earn back his good opinion. "No, you are perfectly right. I should have offered. I didn't think. I will speak to my maid tonight."

"I would appreciate that," Bingley said. "I want

both of the Miss Bennets to be well taken care of."

"And they shall be," Miss Bingley said, glancing at Darcy.

He smiled briefly, trying to imagine her at Pemberley. Would she be a good hostess? For some reason, she did not appear to approve of Miss Bennet, but in general, she knew how to be civil.

"Poor Jane," Mrs. Hurst said later, when they had all migrated to the card table to play silver loo. "She is a sweet, pretty girl and I wish with all my heart that she could be well settled someday."

Bingley frowned. "You speak as if that is an impossibility."

"Given her parents and their low connections, I believe it may be impossible."

Miss Bingley added, "One of her uncles is an attorney in Meryton and another is in business near Cheapside."

Bingley said, "And what does that matter?"

"Oh Charles," Miss Bingley said. "Be reasonable. We are talking about Cheapside."

"I don't care if she has uncles enough to fill all Cheapside. It would not make her one jot less agreeable."

"But it must materially lessen her chance of marrying a man of any consideration in the world," replied Darcy.

"And Miss Eliza Bennet has even lower connections," Miss Bingley said.

Darcy looked at her intently. "What do you mean?"

"She is the daughter of Mr. Bennet's first wife. The current Mrs. Bennet is his second wife. She is the mother of the four younger girls."

Darcy was pleased to hear that she was not related to Mrs. Bennet by blood. "And her mother?"

Miss Bingley paused for dramatic effect. "The daughter of an innkeeper."

Mrs. Hurst gasped. "No."

"Yes, apparently it was a love match." Miss Bingley gave a derisive laugh. "It's difficult to imagine that desultory gentleman overcome by passion, but apparently he was. Mr. Bennet married her in spite of his family's objections."

"I think that is romantic," Bingley said.

"It was foolish," Darcy corrected. No gentleman should marry so far out of his sphere. It would be like him marrying a scullery maid.

"Yes, and that is why Miss Eliza does not have any dowry, although her sisters will have something from their mother. And Mr. Bennet's estate is entailed, so if she does not marry, she will be destitute."

"Unless the innkeeper takes her in," Mrs. Hurst said and they both laughed heartily.

Bingley said sharply, "How do you know all of this? Did they tell you?"

"It is common knowledge, Charles," Miss Bingley said. "I may have heard it from Mrs. Goulding or Mrs. Cole. Everyone knows everything in a small town."

And Miss Bingley has a tendency to gossip, Darcy thought with a twinge of disquiet.

CHAPTER THREE

At breakfast Darcy saw Miss Bennet again. She looked pale and tired. Her hair was again simply styled. He asked about the health of her sister and she smiled briefly, as if grateful for the question.

She revealed that she had been up most of the night with her sister. She wished to invite her stepmother to visit to decide what should be done.

Miss Bingley looked annoyed by the request, but Bingley said, "Absolutely. Whatever she needs. I want — I mean, we all want her to get well as soon as possible." He asked Miss Bennet to write a note for her mother and promised to send a servant to deliver it immediately.

The note was written, the servant was dispatched, and the rest of the party sat down to breakfast.

After expressing her perfunctory concern for Jane, Miss Bingley turned to Mr. Darcy and asked about his daughter and his sister. It's been so long since I've seen them," she said. "Juliette must be quite the little lady now. How old is she now – three?"

"She just turned four."

Miss Bennet looked at him, surprised. "You have a daughter?"

"Yes." On impulse he opened his watch and showed her a miniature portrait. "This is her likeness."

Miss Bennet smiled. "She is a pretty girl."

Miss Bingley insisted on seeing the portrait as well and declared it to be an excellent likeness. "She is the most beautiful little girl, and so clever," Miss Bingley said. "I have never met a child who delighted me so much. When I saw her last, she showed me her doll, even offered to let me hold it. What a sweet, generous heart."

Darcy nodded. "She is a very loving child."

Miss Bennet said, "You must miss her."

"I do."

She looked as if she might say something, but held back.

He said, "What are you thinking?"

She shook her head. "Nothing of importance. Just that I am grateful that my father never travelled far from home. But he lives a quiet life and dislikes

London."

Darcy stiffened. Did she think he was neglecting his daughter? "I assure you, my daughter is well cared for."

"Forgive me, I meant no offense. You obviously have a great affection for her."

"And I would never take her to London; the air is unhealthy."

Miss Bingley, wanting to be part of the conversation, interrupted. "Has Juliette started piano lessons like your sister?"

"I believe she is still very young."

"No doubt she will grow up to be quite like Georgiana." She turned to Elizabeth. "Georgiana is one of the most delightful young women. I long to see her again. Such a countenance, such manners! And so extremely accomplished for her age! Her performance on the pianoforte is exquisite."

Darcy had never realized before how irritatingly effusive Miss Bingley was in her compliments. It made him question her sincerity.

Bingley took a bite of his toast. "It is a wonder to me how all young women can be so accomplished."

"All young women?" Miss Bingley said sharply.

"Yes, for I never meet a young woman without being told that she is accomplished. She either paints tables, covers screens or nets purses."

Darcy said coolly, "True accomplishment requires more than an ability to craft items. In my experience, I do not believe I know more than half a dozen women who are truly accomplished."

"Nor I, I am sure," said Miss Bingley. He had noticed that she almost always agreed with him. He was not certain he wanted a parrot for a wife.

Miss Bennet said, "Then you must comprehend a great deal in your idea of an accomplished woman."

"I do."

"Oh certainly," Miss Bingley added. She proceeded to outline her definition. "A woman must have a thorough knowledge of music, singling, drawing, dancing and the modern languages to deserve the word, and besides all this, she must possess a certain something in her air and manner of walking, the tone of her voice, her address and expression, or the word will be but half deserved."

Darcy wondered briefly if she was attempting to put herself in that category. "And to all this she must add something more substantial, in the improvement of her mind by extensive reading."

He thought of Anne who was always in the process of reading several books.

Elizabeth Bennet said calmly, "I am no longer

surprised at your knowing only six accomplished women. I rather wonder now at your knowing any."

"Are you so severe upon your own sex, as to doubt the possibility of all this?"

"I never saw such a woman."

"Oh, Miss Bennet," Caroline said. "If you frequented Town more, you would find many accomplished women."

She smiled briefly. "Perhaps. Your knowledge is obviously greater than my own. But a more interesting question to me is why gentlemen are rarely called accomplished."

Bingley said, "I believe you are right. I have never been called accomplished."

Darcy smiled. "Do you want to learn how to net purses?"

Bingley laughed good-naturedly.

Miss Bennet added, "When gentlemen are introduced, they are more likely to be described by their wealth or position."

Darcy turned to her. "Perhaps that is because women are most interested in that."

"You think we are mercenary?"

He shrugged. "It is a practical reality. Men control the majority of wealth and power in society and women provide the majority of its grace and comforts. In our social interactions, it is a simple matter of exchange with each trying to make the most advantageous bargain."

Her dark eyes flashed with annoyance. "So you think women are nothing more than pretty baubles."

"I did not say that. I believe that both men and women have a responsibility to improve themselves."

"But you must admit that women are not given the same opportunities as men."

He frowned. "It sounds as if you have read Mrs. Godwin."

"You disapprove?"

"She was an immoral woman."

"Yes, but she made some persuasive arguments."

"I believe a person's character must be judged along with their beliefs."

"Perhaps," she acknowledged. "But none of us, even the brilliant and famous are without flaw. Consider Rousseau. He abandoned his own children. I find that morally reprehensible, but that does not mean I cannot benefit from his wisdom."

Miss Bingley, alarmed at the tone of the conversation, tried to join it. "What a serious conversation for the breakfast table," she joked. "Mr. Darcy, I don't believe you would want your sister Georgiana to read such books."

"Not at age sixteen," he agreed. "But perhaps later, when she is more mature."

"When she has already made the decisions that will determine the course of her life?" Miss Bennet scoffed. "I believe that young people should read more, not less."

For a moment they were both silent and the tension at the table was palpable. Bingley said, "I should read more as well. But I don't make the time. Perhaps if I had an extensive library such as yours at Pemberley, Darcy."

Darcy was grateful for the pleasant turn in the conversation.

"Oh yes," Miss Bingley added. She spoke to Miss Bennet. "Mr. Darcy has the most marvellous library. I believe I could spend ten years in that room and never be bored."

Miss Bennet looked as if she was trying to control her temper. She said to him, "You must have an extensive collection."

Darcy said coolly, "It has been the work of many generations."

Miss Bingley added, "And you have added so much to it yourself, you are always buying books."

"I cannot comprehend the neglect of a family library in such days as these."

Miss Bennet said, "Do you view purchasing new books as a duty or a joy?"

"Both. But I often find that doing my duty is a joy." He frowned as the words came out of his mouth. It was a sincere sentiment, but it made him sound like a prig.

Miss Bennet looked at him thoughtfully but said nothing. A few minutes later, when the meal had finished, she excused herself to check on her sister. She asked that her stepmother be allowed to join them upstairs when she arrived.

After she left, Mrs. Hurst said, "I didn't realize Miss Bennet was such a bluestocking. No wonder she is still unmarried."

Miss Bingley laughed and turned to Mr. Darcy. "I thought for a moment you might come to blows over poor Rousseau."

"Nothing so violent, I assure you," he said smoothly. He did not agree with Miss Bennet, but he had to respect her opinion. And he doubted that Miss Bingley had read enough of the Genevan philosopher to form an intelligent opinion on the man or his theories.

* * *

Elizabeth joined Jane who was sitting up her bed and sipping hot broth. "How was breakfast?" Jane asked.

Elizabeth groaned. "You must try to get better as quickly as possible."

Her sister grew even paler than she was before. "Why? Are they finding our visit irksome?"

"No, not you," Elizabeth said quickly. "Never you. I am the irritating one."

"Surely not."

Elizabeth said, "No, it is true. I don't know what it is, but there is something about Mr. Darcy that brings out the worst in me. He is so stiff and proper. And when he talks, speaking as if he is the fount of all wisdom, it grates on my nerves. I find myself saying outrageous things, just to shake him up, to annoy him further."

Jane sighed. "What did you say?"

"We argued about books. He thinks I should not have read a *Vindication on the Rights of Women*."

"You must admit, it is inflammatory."

"Only to men of small minds."

Her sister smiled. "You don't think that. Mr. Darcy is a well-educated man."

"With an arrogant attitude. You should have heard him talk about censoring his younger sister's reading."

Jane coughed. "Not every young woman has full access to the family library."

"No, and I think it is a shame. How is a woman supposed to be a proper wife and mother if she cannot think for herself?"

"Not everyone wants to be a scholar or to marry one."

Elizabeth smiled. "I know. You are right. But he does annoy me."

"But underneath that, do you like him – just a little?"

Elizabeth laughed. "Like Beatrice with Benedick? Heaven forbid." She couldn't imagine much worse that waking up to his scowl every morning. "No, Miss Bingley can have him with my blessing."

"Miss Bingley?"

"Yes. You should hear her. 'Yes, Mr. Darcy. No, Mr. Darcy. You are so wonderful, Mr. Darcy.'"

Jane shook her head. "Lizzy," she reproved gently.

"Forgive me," Elizabeth said quickly. "I know you are determined to like her. And it is none of my concern what she says to him or how she says it. I just wish I did not have to listen when she flirts with him so outrageously. She grates on my nerves as well."

Within two hours Mrs. Bennet arrived. Elizabeth was glad her stepmother came so she could see Jane, but she brought Kitty and Lydia along as well, which annoyed Mr. Bingley's sisters. Mrs. Bennet did not seem overly concerned with Jane's health. She only stayed upstairs a few minutes, then left to meet with Mr. Bingley and his party. She seemed more interested in admiring Bingley's house and inviting him to dine when Jane was fully recovered. More than once Elizabeth noticed Mr. Darcy's disapproving gaze as he watched her mother. Lydia embarrassed Elizabeth as well by boldly reminding Mr. Bingley that he had promised to host a ball.

Bingley, always the gentleman, said that once Jane was well Lydia could name the day.

Elizabeth was glad when her family left and she could retreat to Jane's bedroom and avoid the Bingleys and their disagreeable houseguest.

* * *

Despite his good intentions, Darcy found himself fascinated by Elizabeth Bennet. Every day she said or did something that surprised him. Caroline Bingley, on the other hand, nearly always said what he would expect her to say.

Miss Bennet spent most of the time with her sister beyond his scope of observation, but when he did see her, she often had a book in her hand. After their conversation at breakfast Darcy wondered at the titles. One evening he noticed as she set one volume aside and chose another. He walked over to the table and casually picked it up, flipping through the pages. He saw that it was the autobiography of Benjamin Franklin. "Are you an admirer of the American Statesman?"

"Yes. Are you?"

"I must admit I prefer his humorous quotes."

They were both invited to join the card table, but Miss Bennet declined.

Mr. Hurst said, "Do you prefer reading to cards? That is rather singular."

"Miss Bennet," said Miss Bingley, "despises cards. She is a great reader and has no pleasure in anything else."

Mr. Darcy stiffened. Perhaps Miss Bingley was trying to tease, but her words had an unpleasant bite.

"I deserve neither such praise nor such censure," said Elizabeth calmly.

"But you think cards beneath your contempt."

Elizabeth smiled. "On the contrary. I enjoy playing cards. I find the mathematical probabilities entertaining, but I fear you may be playing at stakes too high for my purse."

Darcy noticed that she stated her lack of funds in a matter-of-fact manner, without pretence or complaint.

Bingley said quickly, "We shall play for points then, not for money."

"No, please," she said pleasantly. "Do not alter your game for me. I am very happy where I am, reading a novel."

Miss Bingley invited Mr. Darcy to join the card table again, and he did so, if only to increase the distance between himself and Miss Bennet.

The next day he spent more time out of doors, walking in Netherfield's gardens. He also spent an hour in the billiard room. At one point he looked up, surprised to see Elizabeth Bennet in the doorway. How long had she been observing him? He straightened up to his full height. "Can I help you?"

She said, "No, excuse me. I did not mean to interrupt. I must have made a wrong turn somewhere."

She looked delightfully disoriented. "Where do you wish to go?"

"To the gold parlour?"

"To your left."

"Thank you," she said, but stood still for a moment, not leaving. She must have noticed the question in his eyes, for she added, "I thought at first that Mr. Bingley would be here as well. I thought it took two to play billiards."

"That is best. But I often play against myself." Bingley was an inattentive opponent for he did not enjoy the game.

She smiled briefly. "How convenient. Then you always win."

He had never thought of it that way. He said, "Do you know how to play?"

"No, I never learnt. But I assume it is a matter of geometry and the laws of natural philosophy."

"They definitely help." He was about to ask if her she had ever studied Sir Isaac Newton's theories, but Miss Bingley interrupted them. "Oh, there you are, Miss Bennet," she said, her voice almost shrill. "I feared that I had lost you."

Darcy was annoyed by the interruption and briefly wished he could have finished the conversation with Elizabeth. With that thought, he realized that Elizabeth and her intellectual curiosity attracted him much more than he liked.

He needed to steel himself and force himself to think of something else.

He must be on his guard against her.

He returned to the game and scratched a shot. Damn.

* * *

Eventually Jane recovered enough to be able to join the rest of the party after dinner. She was still thin and pale, but her coughing had lessened and she had some appetite. Bingley was very attentive, making certain the fire was piled high enough and making her change her seat so she was farther from the door. He sat beside her and spoke to her in low tones.

Elizabeth watched their interaction with great satisfaction. It appeared that Bingley genuinely cared for Jane.

There were no cards that evening. Mr. Darcy read a book. Miss Bingley tried to interrupt him with conversation, but Elizabeth was amused to see that he gave her no encouragement and answered in the fewest possible words. Mr. Hurst fell asleep on the couch.

Elizabeth busied herself with some needlework.

She glanced once or twice at Mr. Darcy. For a few minutes earlier that day, she had thought they might be able to have a civil conversation, but now he had returned to his standard behaviour – aloof and disapproving.

Elizabeth did not mind. She would be glad when she and Jane were able to return to Longbourn.

Miss Bingley invited her to take a turn about the room. "Do join me. It is so refreshing."

Refreshing would be a walk in the gardens, Elizabeth thought, but acquiesced because she had been sitting for a long time and it would be good to stretch her legs.

She noticed that Mr. Darcy closed his book and looked up at them, which inspired Miss Bingley to ask, "Why don't you join us, Mr. Darcy?"

"No, thank you. I can imagine only two motives for your choosing to walk together and if I joined you, I would interfere with either."

"What can he mean?" Miss Bingley said to Elizabeth. "I am dying to know what could be his meaning. Do you understand him?"

Elizabeth saw an amused look on his face. She said to Miss Bingley, "Not at all, but depend upon it. He means to be severe on us, and our surest way of disappointing him will be to ask nothing about it."

Miss Bingley could not be silent. "I insist that you explain yourself, sir."

Mr. Darcy said calmly, "Either you are in each other's confidence and wish to share a secret, or you are conscious that your figures appear to the greatest advantage in walking. If the first, I should be completely in your way, and if the second, I can admire you much better from where I am sitting."

There was something in his steady gaze that made

Elizabeth blush. He was teasing them, but what if he had been admiring them – admiring her? She felt flushed, as if her skin was tingling. She suddenly felt that her muslin dress was much too thin and wished she had a shawl like Jane.

"Shocking!" Miss Bingley gasped. "I have never heard anything so abominable. How shall we punish him?"

"Laugh at him," Elizabeth said. "Let him know that we don't care what he says."

"Oh, I could never dare laugh at him."

"Too bad. For I enjoy laughing at the follies and weaknesses of others."

"But Mr. Darcy has no weaknesses."

"None?" she said, glancing briefly at the gentleman for his reaction.

Mr. Darcy said, "That is impossible. Everyone has some weaknesses or flaws, but I try to avoid ones that will expose me to ridicule."

"Such as vanity or pride?"

"Does anyone ever consider himself vain?" he asked rhetorically.

"I suppose not."

"And as for pride, I hope I keep mine under proper regulation."

She expected no less from him. He was a proud,

arrogant man, and would never acknowledge his own flaws.

He added, "I do have a temper, though. I don't forgive and forget the way others seem to. My good opinion once lost is lost forever."

She was surprised by his honesty, and looked away, determined to keep the conversation on a lighter tone. "Then I shall be on my best behaviour so I don't incur your wrath."

"You are in no danger of that," he said quietly, then frowned as if he had said more than he intended. He returned to his book, effectively ending the conversation.

CHAPTER FOUR

Darcy dreamed of Elizabeth that night – a strange, tempestuous dream in which he climbed up the wall outside her room and climbed in through the window. She was asleep, her dark hair loose across her pillow, one slim arm above her head. She was lovely. He reached out to touch her, but before he could, he woke.

He pulled up his covers and turned on his side, determined to go back to sleep. Dreams were meaningless, foolishness.

But he could not sleep for thinking of her.

He found it ironic that after all his plans, he dreamt of Elizabeth Bennet instead of Caroline Bingley.

But if he were honest, he was physically attracted to Miss Bennet and not to Miss Bingley.

After a few minutes, he lit a candle by his bedside

and stared at the ceiling.

This was wrong, but part of him wished the dream had lasted a few minutes longer. What would have happened if he had kissed her? Would she have sighed and pulled him closer?

He groaned at the thought of her warm and willing in his arms.

This would never do.

Miss Bennet could never be mistress of Pemberley. She was completely and utterly inappropriate.

He let his breath out slowly, determined to regain his self-control.

A man could not be held accountable for his dreams, but he was accountable for his thoughts and ultimately for his actions.

He refused to think of her, and if he did, he would force himself to think of something else. And he would do everything in his power to avoid her.

* * *

Jane and Elizabeth stayed at Netherfield one more full day, and then rode home in Mr. Bingley's carriage on the following morning. Elizabeth was glad that she had no more uncomfortable conversations with Mr. Darcy. He seemed to ignore her that last day, which was fine with her.

Mrs. Bennet was unhappy to see them. She had hoped that Jane would be able to stay a full week. "But at least your beauty is returning," she said. "You have some colour in your cheeks. Were you able to spend some time with Mr. Bingley?"

Jane hid a cough behind her hand, then answered. "Yes ma'am. He was a most kind and attentive host."

"Excellent. Then it was all worth it," Mrs. Bennet declared. "Now go upstairs and get some rest. We have company for dinner, such as it is." She flashed a look of sharp annoyance at her husband.

Elizabeth turned to her father for explanation. He said, "My cousin Mr. Collins has invited himself to stay a fortnight."

Ah, now Elizabeth understood. Mr. Collins was the man who would inherit Longbourn upon her father's death. They had never met, but Mrs. Bennet could not bear to hear the man's name mentioned.

Elizabeth frowned. "And what is the purpose of his visit?"

"He says he wants to extend an olive branch."

Mrs. Bennet scoffed. "He wants to see what he will inherit and gloat over his good fortune. I think it very cruel for your estate to be settled away from your five daughters and to be given to a stranger."

"But, my dear," Mr. Bennet said reasonably,

"After today, Mr. Collins will no longer be a stranger."

"Oh, Mr. Bennet," she wailed. "You have no heart. If you did, you would have found a way to remove the entail years ago."

Her stepmother did not understand the inevitability of the law. Without a son to inherit, her father could not remove the entail. After his wife had left to supervise the preparation of dinner, Mr. Bennet spoke quietly to Elizabeth. "It is good to have you back, Lizzy."

"It is good to be home," she agreed.

"Kitty," Lydia shouted from an upstairs room. "Have you seen my green slippers?"

Mr. Bennet sighed. "Although you might justifiably wish that you could have stayed longer at Netherfield."

"No, not I," she said truthfully.

"Not even for the peace and quiet?"

She shook her head. She did not mind the noise and bustle of their house, and it was much better than having to be polite to Miss Bingley and Mr. Darcy.

Her father retired to his library, closing the door behind him.

Elizabeth walked up to her bedroom, thinking about Miss Bingley and her pursuit of Mr. Darcy. In a way, they suited each other – they were both proud, disagreeable people. She wondered briefly if Miss Bingley would be successful in getting Mr. Darcy as a husband.

What abominable children they would have, she thought, then laughed at her foolishness.

That evening they all met Mr. Collins. He was a large, stocky man with a dull countenance and formal manners. He seemed overly impressed with his position as a clergyman and the rank of his patroness, Lady Catherine de Bourgh. He spoke of little else. He was full of meaningless complements and flattery, which amused her father and seemed to appease her stepmother. Elizabeth was polite to him as civility demanded, but thought he was a vain, foolish man.

On the third day of his visit he accompanied Elizabeth and three of her sisters on a walk to Meryton. Mary, who had little interest in new bonnets or officers, chose stay home. As they approached the centre of town, Lydia noticed one of the young officers, Mr. Denny, and waved at him.

"Lydia," Elizabeth whispered, wishing her younger sister would not make a spectacle of herself, but it was too late to check her. She and Kitty ran across the street to talk with him.

Elizabeth, Jane and Mr. Collins followed in a

more sedate manner.

As they approached, Elizabeth noticed that Captain Denny was walking with another young man. He was taller than average and handsome with a confident air.

Mr. Denny introduced them to his friend. His name was Mr. Wickham and he had just accepted a commission in their corps.

He had a fine countenance, a good figure and a pleasing address.

He smiled at Elizabeth and asked what her favourite sites in Meryton were.

She was flattered by the attention and would have answered, but they were all distracted by the sound of horses as two riders approached. Mr. Darcy and Mr. Bingley came closer on horseback and spoke to them from their higher position. "Good afternoon, Miss Bennet, Miss Jane," Mr. Bingley said to them both, but his eyes were on Jane. "We were on our way to Longbourn to ask about you. I can see that you must be feeling better."

Jane blushed. "I am feeling much better, thank you."

Elizabeth thought that Mr. Darcy was about to say something, when she saw him catch sight of Mr. Wickham. She saw that they were both surprised.

They obviously knew each other. Both changed colour, one looked white, the other red. Mr. Wickham touched his hat, a salutation that Darcy ignored. He rudely turned his horse away.

Bingley spoke another minute with Jane, and then hurried to join his friend and ride on.

What was that about? Elizabeth thought as she watched the gentlemen retreat.

She glanced at Wickham who shrugged and smiled, as if to say that it was of little importance, and she, not wanting to embarrass him, did not question him. The group of them walked on to her Aunt Philips' house, which was in town. Lydia invited Mr. Denny and Mr. Wickham to join them inside, but they politely declined and said their farewells.

Lydia sighed once the door was shut. "I think I'm in love with Mr. Wickham. Have you ever seen such a handsome man?"

"He'll look ten times better in a uniform," Kitty said.

They both giggled.

Mrs. Philips told them not to worry for she had already planned a dinner for the following night. She would make her husband invite both those officers, if everyone at Longbourn could come as well.

"I will ask my stepmother," Elizabeth said, already

looking forward to the possibility of seeing their new acquaintance again.

Mrs. Bennet had no objections and the next evening found them all in Mrs. Philip's sitting room. The majority of the guests were seated at tables, playing cards, but Mr. Wickham did not play cards. He singled Elizabeth out and sat beside her. "Ah, Miss Bennet. You like me, prefer conversation to cards."

"I suppose that depends on one's partner. Are you enjoying Meryton, sir?"

"Very much. I find the company delightful." His eyes sparkled with admiration for her.

She would have liked to ask him how he knew Mr. Darcy and to explain their strange meeting, but knew it would be too impolite to ask.

Fortunately, he brought up the topic himself. He asked how long Mr. Darcy had been staying at Netherfield.

"About a month."

"Are you well acquainted with him?"

"As much as I'd like to be," she said sharply, then corrected herself. "I am sorry. I spent several days in his company at Netherfield and I find him disagreeable."

"He can be," Mr. Wickham agreed. "He often

thinks himself better than his company. But most people overlook that because of his wealth and position. They flatter him, seeking an advantage."

"I hope I am not so insincere."

"No, I didn't think you would be. You strike me as an honest person."

"I try to be."

He said, "You may be surprised to learn that Mr. Darcy and I grew up together. At one time we were good friends, almost like brothers."

She frowned. "But yesterday –" She caught herself. "Forgive me."

"No doubt you noticed the very cold manner of our meeting." He smiled. "Unfortunately, Mr. Darcy and I are not on the best of terms now."

"That is too bad."

He leaned forward and spoke in a confidential tone. "Although I tried to prevent it, we had a falling out after his father died. You see, my father was the late Mr. Darcy's steward. The late Mr. Darcy took an interest in me and fostered my education. He intended me to go into the church and bequeathed me a living in his will. But later, when the position became vacant, Mr. Darcy refused to honour it."

"Good heavens!" Elizabeth cried. Mrs. Phillips glanced over at her in alarm, so she lowered her voice.

"But how could that be?"

Mr. Wickham said, "There was a vagueness in the terms of the bequest. Mr. Darcy knew what his father intended, but chose to ignore it."

"But why?"

"I believe he has always been jealous of me. He resented the fact that his father cared for me."

Elizabeth could not believe what she was hearing. Mr. Darcy had struck her as an arrogant man but never as a dishonourable one. To think that he could be so revengeful, to commit such an injustice to such a promising young man as Mr. Wickham. "That is abominable."

Mr. Wickham said, "True, but I don't want to upset you. Don't be concerned. I may not be a clergyman, but I have found a new profession as a soldier. Which I find very enjoyable."

She admired his positive attitude.

Lydia interrupted them. "We need a fourth at our table. Will you join us, Mr. Wickham?"

"Gladly, if Miss Bennet will excuse me."

Elizabeth nodded, and Mr. Wickham bowed. She watched him walk away and thought that he was one gentleman she would like to get to know better.

* * *

Netherfield Park was too quiet without the Bennets. Mr. Darcy tried to entertain himself with riding in the mornings, taking long walks and reading, but Bingley's library was limited. When Bingley suggested riding out to Longbourn to make a call on the Bennets, he had agreed. He thought that if he met the Bennets again, particularly Mrs. Bennet, he would be able to extinguish his foolish fascination for Elizabeth once and for all.

He had been surprised to see them in Meryton, and then stunned to see George Wickham again.

George Wickham was a villain and it had taken all his self-control not to expose him as such. He was alarmed to see him talking with the Bennets, smiling at Elizabeth.

That snake.

He wished he could warn her not to trust his smooth civilities, but he did not know how.

Bingley was planning to give a ball at Netherfield. Perhaps he could talk to her then.

* * *

Elizabeth took extra time preparing for the ball at Netherfield. She wanted to look her best and hoped that Mr. Wickham would admire the results. She was surprised when she came into her room to see that

Jane, although dressed, had not had her hair styled. "I thought you were ready."

Jane said, "I rested while Kitty and Lydia had their hair styled and I fell asleep."

"That was wise, considering that we will be awake half the night. But you had better hurry now or Mama will have an attack of her nerves."

Jane covered her mouth to hide a cough. "I know. If you would ask Maggie to come help, I would appreciate it."

Elizabeth could hear the weariness in her voice. "Are you well enough to go to the Ball?"

Jane assured her, "I am fine."

There were faint grey shadows under her eyes. "I don't think you have completely recovered from your cold at Netherfield."

"No, I just have a little cough that won't go away. It is nothing."

"Maybe you should stay home tonight."

"That would be worse. Mama would never forgive me. Besides, I would like to see Mr. Bingley again."

Elizabeth said, "But you don't want to cough on him."

"Don't worry. I won't."

"Even so, I will ask Hill to make you some ginger lemon tea."

Jane smiled. "Thank you."

Eventually Jane did get her hair styled, and the entire family rode to Netherfield in the carriage. Mr. Collins asked Elizabeth for the first two dances and she couldn't think of a way to avoid him unless she announced her decision not to dance at all, so she reluctantly said yes. Her stepmother nodded and smiled at Mr. Collins, which made Elizabeth fear that they had cooked up some sort of plan between them.

Mrs. Bennet made no secret that the one wish of her heart was for all of her daughters to get married advantageously as soon as possible. Elizabeth was afraid that her stepmother was encouraging Mr. Collins to make her an offer.

It would be a prudent choice financially, but Elizabeth had mixed thoughts on marriage. From her observations, she knew that matrimony was a risky endeavour. Most couples started out with hopes and dreams of felicity, but the actuality was far different. So few marriages were happy. And she knew that if she married Mr. Collins, neither one of them would be happy.

The first dance with him was a sore trial for he did not know the dance. He stepped on her toes twice and bumped into the other dancers. It was embarrassing, and she saw Mr. Darcy stare at them with derision. She could imagine what Miss Bingley and her sister were saying.

There was a short intermission between the first and second dance, so she escaped to the refreshment tables where she met her friend Charlotte Lucas.

"How did you enjoy your dance?" Charlotte asked politely. She was several years older than Elizabeth and did not dance often. Mrs. Bennet thought she was too plain to find a partner.

"You must not have seen it."

Charlotte smiled. "I saw some of it."

"Then you already know my answer." Elizabeth sipped a cup of punch. "I cannot believe I agreed to a second dance with that man."

"You don't wish to dance with him?"

"No." She sighed. "But that is not my greatest concern. He has been talking with my stepmother and I am afraid that he is going to make me an offer."

"I hope you will be very happy together."

Elizabeth laughed. "How can you say that? I won't marry him. If he asks, I will decline."

"But why?"

"Charlotte. You have met him. He is a ridiculous man. You have heard him talk about nothing but himself and his position as the rector for Lady Catherine de Bourgh. Marriage to him would be unbearable."

"I believe you are too harsh. Remember, he will inherit Longbourn when your father dies."

"That is an insufficient reason for marriage."

"You may think differently when that day arrives. You might regret refusing him."

"I would regret marrying him much more."

"Truly?" Charlotte asked. "You would not mind if someone else married him?"

"No. Absolutely not. I would be relieved." Elizabeth saw him across the floor, walking towards them. "Oh, no. Here he comes. I am not certain my toes will survive another dance. I would give anything to avoid it."

"Anything?" Charlotte repeated. "Then I shall have to think of suitable compensation."

Elizabeth frowned. "I don't understand."

"I shall take your place."

Elizabeth was dumbfounded. "Are you serious?"

"He's not as bad as you think," Charlotte said quietly and turned with a smile to face Mr. Collins who approached them.

"Miss Bennet," he said formally. "I believe it is time for our next dance." He bent his arm so she could take it and walk with him to the dance floor

"Forgive me, Mr. Collins," Charlotte said,

smoothly interrupting him. "Miss Bennet was just telling me that she overexerted herself during the last dance."

"Oh, my dear cousin," Mr. Collins said with exaggerated concern. "I hope not dangerously so."

Elizabeth said quickly, "I will be fine, but I fear I am not quite ready for another dance."

"And she suggested that I take her place," Charlotte said boldly and rested her hand on Mr. Collins' arm. "If you do not mind, sir."

Mr. Collins was startled and for a moment his mouth gaped open like a fish. But Charlotte looked up at him with a smile and he was flattered. "Why should I mind, Miss Lucas? I am honoured that you would volunteer."

Elizabeth watched the two of them walk towards the dance floor. Charlotte was a better friend than she had realized. She hoped her dancing slippers were thick.

She looked about the room for Mr. Wickham, but although there were many officers in attendance, he was not one of them. Elizabeth was disappointed, for she had hoped to dance with him. She spoke briefly to his friend Captain Denny who said that Wickham had business in town and could not attend.

At Elizabeth's look of surprise, he added

meaningfully, "I believe he would have postponed that business if he had not wished to avoid the presence of one certain gentleman."

Elizabeth disliked Mr. Darcy even more now, for he had significantly lessened her enjoyment of the evening. She wished briefly that she could tell him what she thought of him, and while she was harbouring these negative thoughts, he suddenly appeared before her. Tall and handsome, impeccably dressed in a brilliant white shirt and cravat, grey waistcoat and black evening coat. He wore pantaloons rather than breeches that hugged his muscular legs.

She made herself look up into his cool blue eyes.

"Miss Bennet," he said formally. "Would you do me the honour of dancing the next set with me?"

She was so startled, she said yes before she could think differently, and then he left immediately and she was left to fret over her own want of presence of mind.

What had she been thinking?

CHAPTER FIVE

What had he been thinking? Darcy walked away quickly in an effort to compose himself. He had planned to talk with Miss Bennet, to warn her about Wickham, but when he approached and she looked up at him with those beautiful eyes, he had asked her to dance.

Logically he knew that when they were dancing, he would be able to converse with her without others paying much attention or noticing that he had singled her out. But he knew his true purpose was to be close to her, to have the opportunity to touch her hand and waist, to have her face near his.

He castigated himself for being a fool and tempting fate. He feared that dancing with her would make him desire even greater intimacies.

But he would focus on the task at hand and try not to be overcome by her warm, physical presence.

He set his face into a cool mask and approached her again. She looked at him gravely, no smile on her face. "Mr. Darcy," she said politely and took his hand.

He wished society did not require everyone to wear gloves at a ball. He would like to have her hand in his, flesh against flesh, even if only for a brief moment.

But he would not think of that.

Out of the corner of his eyes he noticed that Bingley seemed surprised as he escorted Elizabeth to the dance floor.

The music began, and Mr. Darcy tried to think of a way to bring up Mr. Wickham's name, but it all seemed so awkward that he said nothing. For a few minutes they danced in silence. He breathed in the scent of her – rosewater and something that was uniquely her.

She had a thin gold chain with a small cross around her creamy neck that rose and fell with her breath. How he would like to press his lips to the spot and feel her pulse.

Enough, Darcy, he thought. You are a man, not a callow youth ruled by your passions. Pay attention to the dance steps.

Elizabeth said, "I believe it is customary for

couples to converse when they are dancing, but perhaps you do not wish to."

His gaze flew up to meet hers. "On the contrary, I would speak, if I knew what to say."

She looked at him consideringly. "It does not have to be of great importance. You could comment on the size of the room or the number of couples."

"Do you wish me to speak of something so obvious and meaningless?"

"Most conversation is both, don't you agree?"

"Then why is it necessary?"

Elizabeth said, "Most people do not want to look odd, remaining entirely silent for half an hour together, but if you do not wish to speak, I will not provoke you any further."

"You do not provoke me." But that was not entirely true, he thought, for she did provoke him. He had never been so stirred by a woman in his life. Dancing with her was sweet torture. In the course of the dance, they stepped forward and back, turned away and then returned, again and again. Each time she was apart from him, he felt the loss, and when she returned, he felt an upsurge of pleasure. He wished Meryton was advanced enough to allow a waltz but feared that having her completely in his arms might overwhelm his senses.

He had never met such a woman. He wanted to talk to her all day and make love to her all night.

He decided that if he was going to talk of Wickham, he should do so quickly. "I was surprised to see you and your sister in Meryton the other day. Your sister is well?"

"Yes, she is almost recovered. Thank you."

"I am sorry I did not stay and join the conversation," he said. "But I was alarmed to see an old acquaintance of mine."

"Mr. Wickham?" she prompted.

"Yes. I must warn you that he is not a man to be trusted."

She looked surprised. The dance separated them for a brief moment, and when they came together again, he said, "He is not an honourable man."

She said nothing.

They performed a few more steps. He said, "Pardon me. Did you hear what I said before?"

"Yes, but I don't know what to think, for Mr. Wickham said the same of you."

Mr. Darcy frowned. He should have expected that. "I don't know what lies he has told you, but I must speak the truth."

"No doubt he believes he is speaking the truth as well. But then there are often two sides to a story."

Darcy knew she was trying to be logical, but it annoyed him that she would take Wickham's side. "Mr. Wickham is a gamester."

"Gambling is a common form of entertainment."

"But he plays beyond his means. He is greatly in debt."

Her beautiful eyes flashed with anger. "Because he did not receive the living your father promised him."

Darcy was dumfounded. "When my father died, Wickham said he did not wish to be a clergyman and was adequately compensated."

She seemed surprised by this piece of information, but said only, "So you say."

He was insulted by her words. Did she think he was lying? "Do you want to see a copy of the receipt?"

They danced for another minute, and he saw the indecision on her face. Was she willing to believe him now?

"Mr. Darcy," she said finally, "It appears that you and he have a different interpretation of the facts. It is not my place to conduct an investigation into your private lives."

"I appreciate that, but I must warn you. Mr. Wickham is a charming man, and more than one woman has learned to her sorrow that he is also dangerous."

"If that were the case, wouldn't his reputation be known?"

Mr. Darcy stiffened. "I am not going to name names."

She nodded, as if willing to consider his words.

He added, "He is completely selfish and immoral. A habitual liar."

"Is he a drunkard, too?"

He was startled by the question. "No, I don't believe he drinks to excess, but he may. Why?"

She smiled. "Because you are painting him as a complete villain. Like someone in one of the marble backed novels. A profligate gamester who seduces women. I wonder what you will say next — is he a murderer as well? Or does he merely kidnap young women and lock them in towers?"

She was not taking his words seriously. "I never said that."

"No, but you have said more than enough to blacken his character."

"It was my intention to warn you. To put you on your guard."

"Then you have done so. Thank you for your concern."

From her closed expression, he knew that she was merely being polite. She did not believe him. He did not know what else to say to her. "Forgive me, Miss Bennet. I meant well."

"Did you?" she asked lightly, then added in a more sombre tone. "From my perspective, I believe you meant to do him ill. As you have done before." She hesitated as if collecting her thoughts, then added, "But your mutual animosity is none of my concern. I wish you both well and that you will someday resolve your differences."

He clenched his jaw. "That is impossible."

"Charity, Mr. Darcy," she said coolly. "I believe it is our Christian duty to extend it to others."

There was no way to make her understand without breaching confidences that he would not betray. The music ended and he bowed low. "I wish only for your health and happiness, Miss Bennet," he said quietly.

She curtseyed. "Sir."

Her tone was as cold as ice.

They separated and he watched as she walked back to her friend Miss Lucas.

He cursed himself for a fool. He was not rational where Wickham was concerned and his hatred for the man had tainted the conversation, making Elizabeth think he was unreasonable and vindictive.

"Darcy," Bingley said, approaching him with a

smile. "I'm glad to see you enjoying yourself."

He was in no mood for polite conversation. "Good night, Bingley. Make my farewells to your sisters. I will see you in the morning."

As he left the ballroom, he felt that Elizabeth might be staring at him, laughing at him, and he refused to turn and look to see if he were correct.

* * *

Elizabeth spoke briefly to Charlotte, who congratulated her on her dance with Darcy. "I believe he likes you, Lizzy."

"Please do not joke about it. He does not approve of me."

"Then what were you talking of so intently during your dance?"

Elizabeth shook her head. "Nothing of importance." She would not repeat his vile accusations. Wickham could not be such a blackguard. Everything about him emphasized his candour and decency. Whereas everything about Mr. Darcy emphasized his pompous conceit. She changed the subject. "And what of your dance with Mr. Collins?"

Charlotte smiled. "Very enjoyable."

Elizabeth laughed. "Liar."

The rest of the evening passed with little drama. Mrs. Bennet did embarrass her by telling Lady Lucas in a loud voice that she hoped to see Jane married and living at Netherfield soon, but fortunately Mr. Darcy seemed to have left the party earlier, so at least he did not overhear her.

They were the last of the party to leave. As they waited for their carriage to arrive, Mr. Bingley spoke to Jane. They stood together, a little detached from the rest. Mrs. Hurst and Miss Bingley complained about being tired.

When the carriage arrived, Mrs. Bennet invited Mr. Bingley to join them for a family dinner. Miss Bingley looked annoyed, but Mr. Bingley promised that he would be happy to come after he returned from London. He was leaving the next day for a short visit. But he promised that would be back within a week.

"Then you shall dine with us a week from this Saturday," Mrs. Bennet said.

"As you wish," he said pleasantly.

Mrs. Bennet was pleased, and on the way home, amused herself by planning the special dishes she would serve. "And I daresay that you'll be married by January," she said to Jane and sighed happily. "I knew you could not be so beautiful for nothing."

Elizabeth had hoped to be able to talk to Jane about the things Mr. Darcy had said about Mr. Wickham when they reached home, but Jane was too tired. "You can tell me everything in the morning," she promised.

The next day Jane was too ill to talk. Her Netherfield cold had returned, stronger than before. Mr. Collins tried to engage Elizabeth in a private conversation, but she told him she was too busy caring for her sister.

"But I have something of a particular nature to ask you. Indeed, I insist on having an audience."

Elizabeth looked about, wondering how she could avoid the conversation, or at least minimize its effects. "Yes, Mr. Collins, if you insist," she said finally. "We can walk in the garden and talk there."

Elizabeth put on a warm pelisse and gloves and they stepped outside. As they walked toward the garden, Mr. Collins began speaking of his patroness Lady Catherine de Bourgh and her suggestion that he marry and find himself a useful woman, not brought up too high, to marry him and become mistress of the parsonage.

Elizabeth cleared her throat. "Mr. Collins, forgive me. I know you have something of importance to say to me, but I must speak first. I do not know if you are intending to propose to me, and indeed it is indelicate of me to even suppose that, but I have noticed your attentions and I wish to save you the pain of a rejection."

Mr. Collins looked flabbergasted. "But, Miss Bennet, considering my position and situation in life—"

She would not let him finish. "Yes, Mr. Collins, I acknowledge that you are an estimable man with many good qualities, but I believe we would not suit. My hopes are engaged elsewhere –" That was not a complete lie, for her hopes were engaged in the possibility of marrying a man she could respect, "And I think you would be much happier with someone who has shown you greater attention." She referred to her sister Mary who seemed to hang on his every word and often tried to get his notice.

"Someone who has shown me greater attention?"

"Yes, all things being equal, would you not rather spend your life with someone who has already shown a partiality for you?"

He frowned, "I had not thought of that."

"Then think on it, please. For I do wish you well and would like you to be happy in your marriage."

"You do not wish to be mistress of Longbourn when your father has died?"

"No, sir. I will gladly give up that opportunity, for I believe that the woman you choose instead will still be in a position to care for my family, will she not?"

He nodded. "Yes, you are right."

Impulsively he took her hand. "Miss Bennet, thank you for your kindness. I will follow your advice."

For a brief moment, she feared that his excess of emotion might lead him to embrace or kiss her, but instead he merely pumped her hand up and down vigorously.

When they came back to the house, Mrs. Bennet looked at her inquiringly and asked if she had anything to say. Elizabeth smiled lightly. "No ma'am," she said and went upstairs to care for Jane.

Lydia and Kitty walked to Meryton and visited their Aunt Philips. When they returned, they reported that Mr. Wickham was there, handsome as ever. They had teased him about missing the Netherfield Ball. Lydia added, "And he specifically asked about you, Lizzy. I told him you were home playing nursemaid."

That afternoon Jane received a letter from Miss Bingley. "Please read it for me," she asked, so Elizabeth did so. Miss Bingley wrote that the entire Netherfield party had left for London. She said that she would miss Jane, but she did not expect any of them to return to Netherfield that winter.

Jane sighed. "What else does she say?"

Elizabeth scanned the letter, silently reading ahead. She frowned as she came across a passage about Miss Darcy, Mr. Darcy's younger sister. *My brother admires her greatly already, he will have frequent opportunity now of seeing her on the most intimate footing, her relations all wish the connection as much as his own, and a sister's partiality is not misleading me, I think, when I call Charles most capable of engaging any woman's heart. With all these circumstances to favour an attachment and nothing to prevent it, am I wrong, my dearest Jane, in indulging the hope of an event which will secure the happiness of so many?*

"What is it?" Jane asked.

"She says that they look forward to spending time with Mr. Darcy's sister."

"Read it to me, completely."

Elizabeth did as she was commanded but quickly added her own interpretation. "I don't think it is as bad as it sounds. Obviously Miss Bingley has noticed that her brother is in love with you and she wants him to marry Miss Darcy."

Jane coughed. "No, you are too kind. Caroline

neither expects nor wishes me to be her sister. She thinks her brother is indifferent to me but thinks I may have misinterpreted his intentions and wishes to put me on my guard."

"No," Elizabeth said firmly. "No one who has seen you two together can doubt his affection. He cares for you, Jane. I know it."

"I think he does, but what if we are both mistaken?"

"You must not think that," Elizabeth said firmly. "He said he would be back within a week, and I think you should trust him. It does not matter what his sisters want. Your primary concern is to get well, so you can spend time with him when he returns."

"I'll do my best," Jane said weakly. "And in the meantime, do not let Mama read the letter."

"I won't," Elizabeth promised.

* * *

Two days later, the majority of the Bennet family dined at the Philips' home and Elizabeth had a chance to speak with Mr. Wickham. She had thought often of her conversation with Mr. Darcy and could not decide which man was more credible. Mr. Wickham certainly had the appearance of being more temperate in his opinions.

And when she saw Mr. Wickham smile at her, she felt that he could not be as evil as Mr. Darcy had painted him. When they were together, she told him, "I did not see you at Netherfield."

"No, I decided that it would be better not to meet Mr. Darcy. I was afraid that if we were in the same room for so many hours together, an unpleasant scene might arise. I admire Mr. Bingley too much to cause him alarm."

"You were wise," she said.

"Did you miss me?"

Elizabeth blushed and looked down. She had missed him.

He lowered his voice. "That was too forward of me. Of course you did not miss me. No doubt you found dozens of willing dance partners."

"Not dozens, but I did dance," she admitted lightly. "And surprisingly, I even danced with Mr. Darcy."

His eyebrows rose. "Your worth has just risen in my regard. Mr. Darcy rarely dances."

"I know, and I am not surprised. For his conversation was most disagreeable."

"In what way?"

She looked him straight in the eye. "He said you were not to be trusted with women."

Wickham shrugged, seemingly unconcerned. "That's a rather damning phrase. Did he give you any particulars so I may defend myself?"

"No, no particulars."

He looked at her as if trying to judge her reaction. "Well, I am not one to bandy a woman's name about, but since the lady in question is dead, I suppose it will do no harm to tell you the sad tale. I trust you will keep my secret in the strictest confidence."

"Naturally."

He glanced about the room to make certain no one was attending to their conversation. "When I was young, Darcy's cousin, the former Miss Anne de Bourgh often visited Pemberley. Her mother is Lady Catherine de Bourgh, the sister of Lady Anne, Darcy's mother. We were great friends as children, but as we grew, she developed a *tendre* for me. I cared for her as well, although my feelings were not as strong, and I knew that her family wished her to marry Darcy so I did not encourage her. But she was a romantic young woman, forever reading Shakespeare. I believe she felt like Juliet, falling for the steward's son."

He smiled ruefully. "One day she approached me in tears, telling me that her family insisted that she marry Darcy. She asked if I loved her and begged me to marry her. What could I do? I was young and chivalrous. I knew her family would not agree, but for her sake, I tried. I approached Lady Catherine who had me horsewhipped and thrown off her property."

Elizabeth gasped. "Oh, no. How terrible."

He sighed. "There was no way to reach Anne. If I could, I would have eloped with her, even if her family disowned her."

His expression was so open, so devoid of pretence. Elizabeth's heart was touched by his tale. "What happened?"

"A few weeks later, I learned that she had married Darcy. I wrote to her, wishing her well, but I'm not certain she ever received the letter. To be honest, I thought it was for the best. She would never have been happy if she were estranged from her family, and I hoped she would come to care for him in time."

"And you?"

"I finished my education and pursued a career. At about this time, Darcy's father died, and I was supposed to be granted a living."

"Darcy said that you had decided not to become a clergyman and were paid a compensation to relinquish the living."

"He would say that." He smiled.

"Are you saying he lied?"

Wickham shrugged. "He tried to bribe me to leave. But I did not take it. I could have sued him at law but chose not to. I didn't want to distress Anne further. I could not do that to her."

"Do you think she still loved you?"

"I don't know. By that time she had a child, and I hope she found some happiness in motherhood."

Elizabeth did not know what to think or how to feel. She wondered if Wickham had truly loved Anne. He seemed heart-whole now, but that could be his cheerful personality, trying to put the past behind him.

He said quietly, "That's the real reason why Darcy hates me. Because his wife loved me."

It all made sense now. No wonder Darcy hated Wickham. And that was why he thought he was a dangerous seducer.

When Elizabeth came home, she wanted to talk to Jane, to tell her all that Wickham had told her, but he had sworn her to secrecy.

She felt as her heart would burst with all the emotional stories she had been told. First Darcy's tale and then Wickham's. But she could not share the first without mentioning the second. She would have to keep all her thoughts and feelings locked up inside.

The day before he was scheduled to leave

Longbourn, Mr. Collins announced his engagement to Charlotte Lucas. Mrs. Bennet was flabbergasted. "But she's not even pretty," she exclaimed. "And I thought you wanted to marry Elizabeth."

Mr. Collins had the grace to look embarrassed, but Elizabeth tried to salvage the conversation by asking about the wedding plans. They would be married before the end of the year. "And my dear Charlotte wants to invite you to Hunsford in the spring," he said in pompous tones. "If you would honour our humble home with your presence."

Jane was going to visit her Aunt and Uncle Gardiner in London during that time, so Elizabeth would enjoy leaving home. "I would like that, thank you," she said.

CHAPTER SIX

Mr. Darcy travelled to London with Bingley's sisters two days after the Netherfield Ball. The ride was tedious with Miss Bingley trying to engage him in conversation and spending most of the time denigrating Miss Bennet.

He wondered if she had singled out that young woman as a target because she had noticed his fascination with her.

If Miss Bingley thought to advance herself as a marriage candidate by making him realize Miss Bennet's flaws, she was mistaken. He already agreed that Miss Bennet was unsuitable and he had no intention of marrying her, but that did not mean he wished to hear about her atrocious relations for hours on end. He tried to change the subject several times and when that was unsuccessful, he merely stared out the carriage window.

In addition, every negative, unkind statement Caroline Bingley made, strengthened his determination to never marry her. He did not want a selfish, self-absorbed wife. He had a feeling that in time Caroline Bingley would become like his mother-in-law, Lady Catherine de Bourgh. One such relation was more than enough. And if he married Caroline, there would be no escaping from her. He decided that it would be better to remain alone the rest of his life than to be shackled to such a shrew.

He still thought of Elizabeth Bennet, but hoped that by separating himself from her sphere of influence, that his peace of mind would eventually return. In the spring he would return to London and search for a more appropriate wife.

That evening, they dined together in a town house Bingley was renting. Bingley asked if they had visited the Bennets before they left.

"There was no need, Charles," Miss Bingley said. "Besides, I would not want to give rise to any expectations by singling her out for attention."

"I hope you are not seriously considering her as your bride," Miss Bingley continued.

Bingley glanced at Darcy. "I don't know what I am considering at present."

Darcy watched as Miss Bingley skillfully persuaded

Charles not to return to Netherfield. At least not until the spring.

Charles waited until they were alone to talk to him privately. "What do you think, Darcy?"

"That is your decision, Charles. Netherfield is your house. If you wish to go back, do. If you don't, don't. Don't let your sister order you about."

"Caroline is concerned about Miss Jane Bennet. She thinks I have shown her too much attention and that she is expecting an offer. What do you think?"

"I imagine that her mother has such plans. She is a grasping woman, determined to see her daughters marry well. But what do you want? Do you want to marry the girl, knowing her relations?"

"I think I do."

Darcy shook his head at his friend's foolishness. "Do not let passion overrule your reason. There is a common phrase – marry in haste, repent in leisure. Think before you act. Marriage is a solemn business, not something to be taken lightly."

"I do love her."

"But you have been in love before. Remember the glorious redhead in Bath? What was her name?"

Bingley coloured. "Miss Hatch, but that was different."

"How?"

Bingley said, "I didn't really know her. I was infatuated. And I don't think she cared for me."

"She didn't. She was looking for a Lord and found ultimately found one."

"But what about Jane Bennet? Do you think she cares for me?"

"I don't think she is mercenary like Miss Hatch, but I don't think she loves you, either."

"Why do you say that?"

"She's a pretty girl, but there is not much there. She has no vivacity, no energy."

"But she loves me."

"I don't think so." Darcy hated to say this but felt that he must. "At the Ball, I watched her. She smiled at you, but overall, she appeared bored. As if she was only there because she had to be. She appeared fatigued by the effort."

"Bored?"

"You can do much better, Charles."

"You think so?"

"I know so. You have been tempted by a sweet girl with a pretty face. It is perfectly natural. But when it comes to marriage, you should act with wisdom and discipline." He felt that he was giving Bingley the advice he needed to give himself.

* * *

A week passed. Mr. Bingley wrote a short note to Mrs. Bennet saying that obligations in town made him unable to attend the family dinner. There was no mention of when he might return.

One week became two, with no further word of Mr. Bingley. Netherfield Park remained empty and there was talk of the housekeeper reducing the staff. Jane stayed in her bed, growing weaker each day. Elizabeth daily sat beside her bed for hours. "Jane, you must make an effort to get well."

"Why? Bingley is not coming back." She lay back down against the pillow and sighed. She did not bother to sit up.

"Who cares about Bingley? If he is so inconsistent, so stupid not to return, he does not deserve you. You should forget him and fall in love with someone else."

"Like you and Mr. Wickham?"

Mr. Wickham was recently engaged to Miss King, a local young lady who had inherited a fortune. Elizabeth had never noticed any partiality on his part for the young woman before she became wealthy, but perhaps she had deceived herself, thinking that his attentions to her meant more than they did.

And she could not blame him entirely. Young men, even handsome ones, must have something to live on. Was it so bad for him to look for love as well as financial advantage in a companion?

She thought of what her mother often said. "It is just as easy to fall in love with a rich man as a poor one."

"If not easier," her father sometimes added wryly.

"I was never in love with Mr. Wickham," Elizabeth said calmly. "I will admit, I was flattered by his attentions, and I wondered if it might lead to something more. But he has not broken my heart. I wish him every happiness in his upcoming marriage."

"So do I," Jane said. "And I am glad to hear that his defection hasn't harmed you."

"No. I am just as I was before." Elizabeth took her sister's hand. "And I want you to be the same as well. Forget Bingley."

Jane sighed. "I don't want to forget him."

"Do you really love him, Jane?"

"Yes, even if he doesn't love me." With these words Jane cried, but crying made her cough.

"He's not worth your tears, Jane," Elizabeth said fiercely. At that moment, she thoroughly disliked the young man for causing her sister pain. She hoped that Mr. Bingley and his horrible friend would never return to Netherfield.

In the morning Jane was gone. She had died in her sleep.

The doctor said it was the result of her cold and an inflammation of the lungs, but Elizabeth felt that her illness had been aggravated by her broken heart. If Bingley had returned, Jane would have made more of an effort to live.

Mrs. Bennet was inconsolable. Her oldest daughter, her dearest child, was dead. She refused to dress and spent days in her sitting room, still in her dressing gown, pacing and wailing. Her father, equally grieved, became even more silent and retreated to his library.

Elizabeth cried, but inside she felt hollow, as if Jane had taken all of life's joy with her. With neither of her parents taking control of the situation, the decisions of the burial and services fell to her. Her father's words were terse. "Do what you think best, Lizzy, for I do not have the heart for it."

Lydia cried too, but more for the rules of mourning than the loss of her sister. "I hate wearing black. And why can't I go to parties?" she demanded. "Jane wouldn't want me to be cooped up in the house forever."

"In two months, you can start going to dinner parties."

"But when can I dance?"

Elizabeth felt as if she would never want to dance

again, but knew that was an extreme response. "Within three months. If you do it sooner, people will talk."

Lydia said, "People are stupid. I don't know why society has such rules. Why can't I enjoy myself?"

Elizabeth saw Wickham at the funeral. He spoke to her briefly. "Let me tell you how greatly I will miss your sister. She was one of few truly kind women I have ever met."

Elizabeth nodded. "Thank you."

"You must be especially bereft. You and she were very close."

Elizabeth's throat closed up so she could hardly speak. "Yes. I have lost my dearest friend."

He took her gloved hand in his. "Promise me that if you ever wish to talk about her or share your grief that you will speak to me."

She was stunned by the warmth in his expression.

He said sombrely, "I have lost all my family, and I know how lonely it can be. If you need a friend, let me be your friend."

She nodded. "I appreciate that."

He still held her hand. "I am not just saying polite platitudes. I am sincere. I know it is difficult in today's world for men and women to be true friends."

"Without those with small minds thinking the

worst."

He nodded. "But I defy them and their foolish restrictions. I will be your friend, Elizabeth."

She noticed that he had used her Christian name.

He added, "If you ever want to go for a long walk, let me know. Or we could meet in Meryton."

He meant well, but she could not impose on his good nature. She pulled her hand back. "Thank you, but I think your fiancé might not approve."

He glanced briefly at Miss King who was speaking to the minister and then returned his gaze to her. "Have I disappointed you?"

Elizabeth was surprised by his honesty. "No, I wish you and Miss King every happiness."

His eyes were warm as he said, "Thank you."

* * *

The Gardiners had come for Christmas and stayed for Jane's funeral. Mrs. Gardiner noticed Elizabeth's conversation with Mr. Wickham at the funeral and later asked about him. "Is he a beau of yours, Lizzy? Lydia told me some of his history. He seems ideally situated for a romance – tall, and good looking, having overcome misfortune."

Elizabeth told her that he was engaged elsewhere.

"Too bad. Have you met any other promising

young men?"

She thought briefly of Mr. Bingley, who should have come back for Jane, and his friend Mr. Darcy whom she hoped to never see again. But she would not call Mr. Darcy a young man, for although he was probably only thirty years of age, he had a seriousness that belied the description of "young." "No one of importance," she said finally.

When it was time for the Gardiners to return to London, they offered to take her in the place of dear Jane.

Elizabeth declined. "I would not be good company at present."

"I know, and I am sorry. I hoped that a change of scenery would improve your mood."

"I don't believe I will ever be happy again."

Mrs. Gardiner shook her head. "You feel that now, but life goes on. When my youngest died, I wished I could die as well, but I had other children, other obligations. I needed to take care of them. By doing what was required, even when it was very difficult, I eventually found peace. It will not come quickly, but eventually you will be at peace, too."

"I don't want to be at peace. If someone should die, why not me instead of Jane? Jane was so good."

"Then perhaps Heaven is best for her."

"Don't try to console me with religion. I am not at peace with God right now."

Mrs. Gardiner nodded. "I understand."

Elizabeth appreciated her kindness, but sensed that she would grieve her sister's death for a long time.

* * *

Darcy spent Christmas at Pemberley. He would have gone to Rosings Park, so Lady Catherine could spend time with Juliette, but the weather was bad and Juliette had caught a cold. He would not travel when she was ill, so he arranged to visit at Rosings at Easter. That would interrupt his plans to spend the season in London, searching for a wife, but he could go to Town later in the summer, or put it off for another year entirely. He found that after his emotionally taxing visit to Netherfield, he was not in a hurry to get himself hitched.

* * *

In March Elizabeth prepared for her trip to Hunsford to visit the Collinses. Mr. Bennet spoke to her in the library before she left. They sat in comfortable chairs before the fireplace. He gave her several pound notes for spending money. "Thank you, sir, but you need not. My allowance is sufficient."

"Nonsense. You may want to buy some frippery in town, and I would not begrudge you any pleasure."

"I am not Lydia."

"No, thank goodness." He sighed. "With you gone, the house will be devoid of sense until you return."

"In truth, I would rather not go."

"You still miss Jane."

"Yes, and I find it difficult to be pleasant in company. It feels wrong to be happy and lighthearted when I am still grieving."

He nodded. "I felt the same when your mother died. But you needed a mother, so I looked for a wife. I sometimes think I should have waited another year."

Elizabeth did not want to discuss the wisdom of his choice. That was not her place. "Tell me about my mother," she said instead. "You rarely speak of her, and I don't wish to pry if your feelings are too tender. But I wish I could have known her."

Mr. Bennet stared into the fireplace for a minute, and she thought he might not answer at all, but he finally said, "If you wish to know her, look in a mirror. You are almost her equal, although I think you are a little taller."

Elizabeth prompted, "And her personality?"

"Warm and clever like you." He smiled, remembering. "And her laugh. There was nothing better than when she laughed at one of my jokes. She made me feel brilliant. She made me want to conquer the world. I would have done anything for her."

Elizabeth was silent, thinking that someday she would like a man to feel the same about her.

"But that wasn't all. She was honest and intelligent. We had conversations about things that mattered, not the latest fashion or the furniture in Mrs. Goulding's sister's parlour."

Elizabeth waited.

"Be wise when you marry, Lizzie," he said finally. "And make certain you respect and admire your partner. Fortune is nice, but it can be a cold bedfellow if true affection is not there."

"I have no plans to marry at present," Elizabeth said.

"You should," Mr. Bennet said. "For I will not live forever, and I would like you to be taken care of. I regret that I was not more frugal earlier. I should have set aside more for your future, but I thought I would have a son."

"Do not worry for me, Father. I will be fine."

He smiled. "Who knows? Perhaps you will meet your Prince Charming in Hunsford."

She thought of the fairy tales he had read to her when she was a child. "I do not want a mere prince, father. I am looking for an emperor."

He laughed. "As you should." He rose and kissed her cheek. "Come back quickly, Lizzy. I will miss you."

* * *

For the past few months, Elizabeth had often felt guilty for inadvertently suggesting Charlotte Lucas as a possible wife to Mr. Collins. When she had told him to marry the woman who paid more attention to him, she had thought he would marry her sister Mary, but he, thinking of the ball at Netherfield, had thought she meant Charlotte. She feared that Charlotte who was getting older and felt like a burden to her family had accepted him under duress and would regret her choice once the deed was done, but it appeared that was not the case. Once she was in Hunsford, Elizabeth was surprised to find that her intelligent, capable friend was happily married to her cousin Mr. Collins.

How anyone could be happy with such an irritating man, she did not know.

No doubt Jane would have said something about everyone being different. Elizabeth thought it was more a matter of Charlotte having low expectations.

As far as she could see, Charlotte tended to ignore her husband as much as possible and focused instead on her new home. It was neat and comely, and Mr. Collins spent the majority of his time in his study or visiting Lady Catherine de Bourgh. "We normally dine with her once or twice a week, but not at present, when her son-in-law and granddaughter are visiting."

Elizabeth caught her breath. "Mr. Darcy is visiting?"

"Yes, with his sister Miss Georgiana Darcy and his cousin Colonel Fitzwilliam. While they are here, Lady Catherine will not invite us, for she wants to spend every possible minute with them. She dotes on her granddaughter. I believe she will invite us later, when they have left."

Elizabeth was relieved that she would not have to face Mr. Darcy again. "Will they be here long?"

"Only two weeks more."

Two weeks was not long, Elizabeth told herself. She supposed she could endure being in the same county as Mr. Darcy without losing her composure.

Ten days later Elizabeth was walking in the woods when she saw a little girl playing with rocks by a stream. Elizabeth could see a family resemblance to

Mr. Darcy. The girl had the same dark hair and there was something familiar about her eyes. She was wearing an expensive dress, but no shoes. Elizabeth looked, but did not see a nursemaid or servant of any kind accompanying her. It looked as if the child had escaped from the big house. "Hello," she said quietly, hoping not to startle her.

"Hello," the little girl said matter-of-factly, continuing on with her task: lining up a row of pebbles.

"What are you making?' Elizabeth asked.

"It is a house," the girl said. "This is a parlour, and this," she pointed to a small green leaf, "is a bed."

Elizabeth squatted down so that she was beside her. "A house for what?"

"For a fairy."

"Will you need a roof?" Elizabeth asked.

"No. Fairies don't mind the rain."

Elizabeth nodded. She asked calmly, "Does your nurse know you are here?"

The little girl shook her head. "No, she is napping."

"Don't you think it would be wise to return before they miss you?"

"They won't miss me," the girl said.

"Your father will miss you."

This seemed to affect her. The girl looked worried now. "Perhaps I should go back." She looked around. "Oh, no. I don't know the way back."

"Then I will help you," Elizabeth offered.

She took her small hand and walked with her back towards Rosings.

As they approached, they saw a servant working in one of the gardens. "Miss Darcy!" the man gasped. "What are you doing out?"

The girl hid behind Elizabeth's skirts. She knew she was in trouble.

"I must speak to Mr. Darcy," Elizabeth said. "Would you please tell him I am here in the garden with his daughter?"

The man hurried to the main house.

In a few minutes she saw Mr. Darcy striding towards them, followed by a young servant woman who ran to keep up with him. His face was dark. "Juliette!" he shouted.

Juliette shrank back but said bravely, "Sir?"

"How many times have I told you not to wander off by yourself!' he said fiercely. "You don't know these woods. It isn't safe."

"Where was she?" he demanded of Elizabeth.

"By the stream."

His face grew pale. "She could have —"

"Yes," Elizabeth interrupted before he could say the word 'drowned.' "But she is safe and well. A little dirty, perhaps, but that is to be expected after building a stick house."

He took Juliette's hand and gave it to the young servant woman. "Take her back to the nursery," he said sharply. "And I'll talk to you, Juliette, after you've washed and eaten."

"Yes, sir," she said weakly. "I am sorry, Papa."

His jaw tightened. "I would rather have obedience than an apology," he said coolly. "I will speak with you later."

He motioned for the servant to take Juliette back to the house. He watched their progress for a moment, then turned to Elizabeth.

"Miss Bennet," he said formally. "I owe you my deepest thanks for finding my daughter and bringing her safely back."

"Do not be angry with her, please." Elizabeth said quickly.

He frowned at her. "I won't be. My anger will be elsewhere, for the maid that should have been watching her."

"Your daughter said her nurse was napping."

"My daughter should have been napping."

"At age four?" Elizabeth said with surprise. "Few

children can endure a nap by that age. As for myself, I believe I gave up naps when I was three. The world was much too exciting." She smiled at the memory. "I suspect that your daughter was bored and went exploring. I also played with sticks and rocks."

From the look on his face, Elizabeth decided that she had spoken too much. "Forgive me, it is not my intention to question your parental authority. And you must want to return to the house."

He nodded. "Yes, I do wish to return," he said stiffly. "Thank you again, Miss Bennet. I am forever in your debt. Now, if you will excuse me, I will take my leave."

He bowed slightly as did she. "Good day, Mr. Darcy," she said.

For a few minutes she watched him walk back to Rosings, and then she turned to return to the parsonage. She could tell that Mr. Darcy cared for his daughter, but she feared he might be a harsh disciplinarian. She felt sorry for Miss Juliette to have lost her mother and to only have one parent. But that was none of her concern. She quickened her pace as she walked, so she would not be missed as well.

CHAPTER SEVEN

That evening, Lady Catherine invited the Collinses and their guests to dinner. Mr. Collins was gratified by her condescension and explained, "She wishes especially to thank you, Miss Bennet, for saving her granddaughter."

"I did very little," Elizabeth said. "But I am glad the girl is safe, back with her family."

Mr. Collins told Elizabeth to wear her best dress and not to worry if it was not as fine as the gown worn by Lady Catherine de Bourgh or Miss Darcy. "Her ladyship likes to see the distinctions of rank to be preserved."

Charlotte gave her some advice as well. "Do not mention Jane and her recent death," she said quietly. "After the death of her daughter last year, Lady Catherine is overly sensitive to the topic."

"I don't blame her," Elizabeth said. She would

prefer not to discuss her loss, either. Charlotte was a good friend, but she could not replace Jane. And talking about Jane just made her miss her more.

The main rooms of Rosings Park were grand and with decorated with an abundance of gold leaf and enormous paintings with classical themes – battle scenes and scenes from Greek mythology. Elizabeth wondered if Prometheus having his liver eaten by an eagle was appropriate decoration for a dining room, but thought that it might make one's dinner seem better by comparison.

Mr. Darcy was there, looking solemn. His sister, Miss Darcy, was a tall, handsome young woman, also very quiet. She appeared to be about Lydia's age, but seemed shy and overwhelmed by the company. She spoke if addressed directly, but said little else. In contrast, their cousin Colonel Fitzwilliam was a friendly, open man with amiable manners and a steady stream of pleasant conversation.

Lady Catherine de Bourgh was a tall, large woman, dressed entirely in black. She was a formidable woman with a stern voice. She provided most of the conversation at the dinner table, giving advice on every subject. After dinner, after the coffee came in, she turned to Elizabeth. "Tell me about yourself, Miss Bennet," she demanded.

"What would your ladyship like to know?"

"I understand that you live at Longbourn and your father's estate is entailed upon your cousin Mr. Collins."

"Yes, ma'am."

"Although that is a fine thing for Mr. and Mrs. Collins, I do not believe in entailments. Rosings Park would have gone to my daughter Anne if she had lived, but now it will pass to my granddaughter, Miss Juliette Darcy, just as it should." She changed the subject abruptly. "Do you play and sing, Miss Bennet?"

"A little."

"Then perhaps one of these days, we shall be pleased to hear you. But tonight I believe we will hear Miss Darcy play. She has had extensive lessons with the best masters. You can help her by turning her pages."

Miss Darcy had the grace to blush at her aunt's rudeness. Elizabeth was merely amused. She thought that Mr. Darcy and his mother-in-law had that in common. "Yes, ma'am," she said. She followed Miss Darcy to the pianoforte.

As Miss Darcy played a complicated piece by Handel, Lady Catherine talked to Mrs. Collins about her recent order at the butcher's shop.

When Miss Darcy finished, Lady Catherine said, "That's very good, child."

Miss Darcy dutifully returned to couch and sat by her brother who flashed her a quick smile as if to say, "well done."

Lady Catherine reminded Miss Darcy to practice every day, then turned to Elizabeth. "How many sisters do you have, Miss Bennet?" Her ladyship continued. "I believe Mr. Collins said there was quite a number of you."

"There are four of us," Elizabeth said.

Mr. Darcy looked at her enquiringly.

"No, that's not right," Lady Catherine said. "I distinctly remember he said five."

Mr. Collins sputtered, not knowing what to say, so Elizabeth said quietly, "There were five ma'am, but my eldest sister Jane recently died."

"What did she die of?"

"A severe cold, ma'am. The doctor said it went into her lungs."

Lady Catherine sighed. "That is the way of it. Was she of a frail constitution, your sister?"

"Not particularly."

Lady Catherine shook her head. "Then your doctors are to blame, or your sister for not following their advice. Young people are determined to do what they wish and ignore the advice of their elders. My daughter Anne would have been alive today if she had followed my advice."

Elizabeth glanced briefly at Mr. Darcy to see how he took this information, but his face was expressionless, set as if he had heard this theory before.

Lady Catherine continued, "I told her to wear a shawl every day, no matter what the weather. Drafts, Miss Bennet, they will kill us all. It is only by the grace of God that I am still alive to help with her daughter, Juliette."

"She seems to be a very bright, happy child," Elizabeth said, hoping to shift the focus of the conversation.

"She is the image of her mother," Lady Catherine said. "Sometimes it breaks my heart to see her. I wish you could have known my daughter Anne," she continued, and dabbed at her eyes with a lace handkerchief. "As you can see, I have not removed my mourning. In fact I may never remove it. Unlike her husband who has chosen to return to his normal attire." She sent a look of annoyance at Darcy, then demanded, "Darcy. Tell Miss Bennet about Anne for I am too distraught."

Darcy looked pained, and Elizabeth could not tell

if it was from the memory of his dead wife or irritation at his mother-in-law for belabouring the point, but he dutifully answered, "Like you, Miss Bennet, she liked to read."

Elizabeth wondered what he had felt for his wife. Had he loved her, or had it merely been a marriage arranged to combine their fortunes?

"Tell her about her drawings.," Lady Catherine said.

"My wife also liked to draw," Mr. Darcy said simply.

"Fitzwilliam," Lady Catherine addressed the Colonel. "Fetch the framed portraits in the morning room. You will be amazed by her talent, Miss Bennet."

"Indeed," Mr. Collins interjected. "If only her health had permitted it, she would have been one of the most accomplished young women in all of England."

"Did you know her, sir?" Elizabeth asked, surprised.

"No," Mr. Collins admitted. "But from what I have heard, I truly regret that I did not have the opportunity."

Colonel Fitzwilliam left and then returned to the salon with two framed portraits. One presumably of

Lady Catherine and one of Mr. Darcy. Neither were good representations, but Elizabeth did not want to be unkind. "Your daughter seems to have excellent taste, ma'am," she said finally. It was a politic complement.

Lady Catherine nodded, pleased. "She did. She was the most promising young woman. It was a tragedy for her to be cut down in the prime of her life. I don't know how I will bear it, but at least I have her daughter. I wish I could see Juliette more often. In fact, I keep telling my son-in-law that he should leave her with me. I would make certain that she had a nurse who would not take naps."

Elizabeth saw a flicker of tension in Mr. Darcy's jaw and guessed that that he was offended by his mother-in-law's jab, but he was too polite to verbally acknowledge it.

"Perhaps Miss Juliette needs a governess," Elizabeth suggested, trying to change the subject.

"A governess?" Lady Catherine said. "Surely she is too young for that."

"But she is a bright child and might enjoy the intellectual exercise. I could read by the time I was four. Miss Juliette might be able to as well."

Mr. Darcy seemed interested in her words. "How did you come to read so early?"

"It was my father. He read aloud to me for years while I sat on his lap. He pointed to the words and somehow I learned without formal instruction."

"I don't believe that is wise," Lady Catherine interrupted. "Too much knowledge too soon can agitate a child's brain. And it is best if learning is done in a logical, orderly fashion. I would not want my granddaughter taught in a slapdash manner."

Darcy ignored his mother-in-law. "What were some of the titles you enjoyed as a child?"

"I enjoyed Robinson Crusoe, but I was older then. My father had several books of histories and bible stories. And of course Sandford and Merton." Elizabeth smiled. "I will give you a list, if you would like."

"I would appreciate it, thank you."

At that moment, Mr. Darcy seemed almost as amiable as Mr. Bingley had been.

Lady Catherine, sensing that she was being ignored, interrupted and mentioned books that she had read to her daughter Anne, and the conversation turned back to Mr. Darcy's wife and remained there for the remainder of the evening.

* * *

Elizabeth was sitting by herself the next morning reading a letter, while Mrs. Collins and Maria were gone on business into the village, when she was startled by a ring at the parsonage door. As she had heard no carriage, she thought it not unlikely to be Lady Catherine, but when the door opened, to her very great surprise, Mr. Darcy and Mr. Darcy only, entered the room.

He seemed astonished too on finding her alone and apologized for his intrusion.

They then sat down. Elizabeth asked about his daughter and sister. Both were well.

Mr. Darcy said, "I hope I am not interrupting you."

"No," she said. "I was merely rereading a letter."

"From your family?"

"Yes, but not as you expect. This is one of the letters from Jane, from last year. I brought it with me."

"You must miss her."

"I do, for now I have no one to write to. I could write to my parents, but neither would respond with more than a line. They are poor correspondents. Jane was a true friend as well as sister. She was the keeper of all my secrets."

"Perhaps one of your sisters will take her place."

"Impossible, for none of them have her sweet disposition. I shall have to look elsewhere for a confidante."

"And one day you will marry."

Elizabeth frowned. "I don't take your meaning, sir."

He drew his chair a little towards her and said, "Shouldn't your husband be your closest confidante?"

Elizabeth was surprised by the question, and it appeared that he was surprised by it as well. The gentleman seemed to experience some change of feeling; he drew back in his chair.

Elizabeth strove for humour. "Ideally, you are correct. One's spouse should be one's confidante. But there will always be need for a third party, when one wants to complain about one's spouse."

"I don't believe you would make your husband a topic for idle gossip."

She flushed at his serious tone. "I should hope not. But since he does not exist yet and is merely a figment of my imagination, I can still laugh at him."

And then their short conversation ended with the entrance of Charlotte and her sister, just returned from their walk. The *tete a tete* surprised them. Mr. Darcy explained that he had mistakenly thought they would all be at home. He sat a few minutes longer without speaking, then went away.

"What can be the meaning of this!" Charlotte said

as soon as he was gone. "My dear Eliza, he must be in love with you, or he would never have called on us in this familiar way."

"You are mistaken," Elizabeth said quickly. "For he hardly spoke three words to me all together."

For the next few days, Mr. Darcy and his cousin called at the parsonage, sometimes together or separately. Mr. Darcy did not say much, but he appeared to be watching Elizabeth with an earnest steady gaze. She thought both men must want to avoid Lady Catherine and that they were eager to take any opportunity for leaving the house. Juliette was not the only one who wanted to escape.

She also met Mr. Darcy on several occasions as she walked around the grounds of Rosings Park. She thought after the first time that he would have observed her pattern of walking and tried to avoid her. But to her surprise, he did not. Instead, he often changed his direction and accompanied her, although he still said little.

On one occasion, she walked in Rosings Park but was joined by Colonel Fitzwilliam, rather than Mr. Darcy. She asked how soon they were planning to leave Kent, and he joked about not knowing the exact date, for he was at Darcy's disposal and Darcy had already postponed leaving once.

Elizabeth said, "He must be enjoying his stay at Rosings."

"That I do not know. He appears quieter than usual, more deep in thought."

"That surprises me, for he seems the same as he was when visiting my neighbour Mr. Bingley. Is he normally more talkative and lively?"

"I think so, but that could be based on our years of acquaintance. I assume he is more comfortable with me."

"But Mr. Bingley is one of his good friends, so wouldn't he be equally at ease with him?"

"I suppose so, but perhaps he was concerned for Mr. Bingley."

"I don't understand."

"No, you wouldn't, and it is merely conjecture on my part. Darcy had mentioned performing a service for one of his friends recently, and from his comments I assumed that he was referring to Mr. Bingley."

"A service?" Elizabeth prompted.

"Yes, he said he had recently intervened, saving a friend from a most inconvenient marriage. I assumed it was Bingley because they had been together last summer and Mr. Bingley seems to be the sort of young man to get into a romantic scrape of that kind."

Elizabeth felt her blood run cold. "Did Mr. Darcy give you his reasons for this interference?"

"I understood that there were some very strong objections against the lady."

Elizabeth stiffened. She should have known that Darcy had been the reason Mr. Bingley had stayed in London. But she lifted her chin and made herself smile. "Now you have piqued my interest, sir," she said archly. "I wonder which of my acquaintances might have been the inappropriate object of Mr. Bingley's attentions."

"Oh, no," the Colonel said quickly. "I should have said nothing at all. I was not thinking that you might know the young lady."

Or be related to her, Elizabeth thought. Poor Jane was dead, but she did not want her name bandied about. "I don't think I do," she said firmly. "I think many young women in Meryton found Mr. Bingley amiable, but I don't think anyone set their cap at him. At least none that I noticed. Perhaps Mr. Darcy was referring to another gentleman."

"Perhaps," the Colonel said lightly, "And do forgive me if our conversation bordered on gossip. Please forget that I even mentioned it."

"Done," Elizabeth said, trying to match his tone.

But inwardly she knew she would never forget it. She had thought that Mr. Bingley's sisters had changed his mind, preventing him from returning to Netherfield. But now she knew that Mr. Darcy had been the author of Jane's misery.

The two of them returned to the parsonage and the Colonel expressed his wish of seeing her later that evening at dinner. But Elizabeth was too agitated from his disclosures to dare spending time with any of them that evening. She claimed to have a headache, said she was unwell, and stayed at the parsonage.

As she was resting, she was roused by the sound of the door-bell. At first, she thought it might be Colonel Fitzwilliam who had once before called late in the evening, but to her utter amazement, she saw Mr. Darcy walk into the room.

He briskly asked about her health. She said she was doing a little better.

He sat down for a few moments, and then stood up and walked about the room. Elizabeth did not know what to say, so she remained silent.

After a silence of several minutes he came towards her in an agitated manner and thus began, "In vain have I struggled. It will not do. My feelings will not be repressed. You must allow me to tell you how ardently I admire and love you."

Elizabeth's astonishment was beyond expression. She stared, coloured, and was silent.

Mr. Darcy continued. "After the death of my wife, I knew I must marry again, so it has been on my mind. I had a mental list of what I was looking for, and you have made me disregard it entirely. I know that my love for you is not logical, and my friends and family will think I have gone mad, but I love you so desperately, I no longer care. I know your family and connections are inferior to my own. I know you have no dowry. Lady Catherine will be furious to think that I have replaced her daughter with you. And my uncle the Earl of Matlock may refuse to invite us to his home. But I hope that you and I will be so happy together that their disapproval will not matter. Please, Miss Bennet, make me the happiest of men and accept my hand."

Elizabeth was amazed by his arrogance, but she forced herself to answer him with restraint. "Sir. In such cases, I know I should express my appreciation for the sentiments avowed, but I cannot thank you. I have never desired your good opinion, and until this moment, I had no idea that you thought of me at all. I am sorry to give you pain, but I must decline your offer."

His face grew pale and it appeared that he was struggling for composure. "And this is all your reply? You have no explanation for your rejection?"

Elizabeth felt her anger flare. "If you insist, I will explain. How could I marry a man who ruined my sister's happiness?"

Mr. Darcy changed colour, but he listened without attempting to interrupt her.

"She died, Mr. Darcy, and on her deathbed, she cried about Mr. Bingley, thinking that he had never loved her, that she had mistaken his regard, but the truth was that you were the one who divided them. Mr. Bingley is still at fault for letting himself be persuaded, but what were your motives? Did you know that you were breaking the heart of the kindest, sweetest girl in the world just because her family was not as high as your own? Mr. Bingley's fortune came from Trade. Why couldn't he marry a gentleman's daughter? And what concern of it was yours how he should be made happy? Why were you to be the judge?"

Mr. Darcy said, "I had no idea. I did not think she cared for him. At the Netherfield Ball, she did not smile unless he was looking at her. She appeared bored."

"She was ill, Mr. Darcy. She never recovered from

her chill she first received at Netherfield. It took all of her efforts to attend that dance, and even so, she went only to see Mr. Bingley again."

His face paled. "Then I was mistaken."

"Yes."

"But it was an honest mistake. Based on rational observation."

Elizabeth's ire rose. "You think you know everything, but I am not surprised. From the moment I met you, your manners have shown your arrogance, your conceit, and your selfish disdain for the feelings of others. Your treatment of Mr. Wickham –"

Mr. Darcy interrupted. "I told you before of my dealings with him."

"But not all," she said. "You did not tell me the true reason for your hate. Your poor wife. What was it like to marry a young woman knowing that she loved another?"

He seemed stunned. "Are you referring to Anne?"

"Mr. Wickham told me how she begged him to marry her. To save her from marrying you."

"And you believe his lies?"

"Why is it always lies, Mr. Darcy? Do you think that every time someone disagrees with you or thinks poorly of you that it is a lie? Do you think I am a liar?"

"I think you have foolishly believed the lies of others."

"But what of things I have seen with my own two eyes? I have seen the way you judge others. You made no effort to be civil in Meryton. You are a stern, opinionated man. Even with your own daughter. I heard you yell at her. If you were a loving parent, you would have taken the child in your arms. But no, instead, you sent her to the nursery to await your punishment. You have no heart."

"And this," cried Darcy as he walked with quick steps across the room, "is your opinion of me! This is the estimation in which you hold me. You think I am an ogre with no redeeming virtues."

The harshness of his words cut through her anger. "I refuse to think that anyone has no redeeming virtues, but yours are well hidden. Suffice it to say that you are the last man in the world that I could marry."

"You have said quite enough, madam. I perfectly comprehend your feelings and have now only to be ashamed of what my own have been. Forgive me for having taken up so much of your time." He bowed stiffly and with these words he hastily left the room.

Elizabeth heard him the next moment open the front door and quit the house.

She sank down upon chair, her thoughts in a terrible tumult.

She cried for a few minutes from the strength and distress of her feelings. That she should receive an offer of marriage from Mr. Darcy. It was unbelievable. To think that he had loved her for so long, loved her enough to disregard all his objections? She would be flattered if his prior feelings and actions had not been so offensive.

She could never love him.

CHAPTER EIGHT

The next morning, Elizabeth woke, agitated, her thoughts still consumed by Mr. Darcy and his declaration. She resolved to take a walk after breakfast in the hope that air and exercise would calm her mind.

But on the walk, she met with Mr. Darcy again. He held out a letter, which she instinctively took, and said, "I have been walking in the grove some time in the hope of meeting you. Will you do me the honour of reading that letter?"

She agreed, he bowed and turned again back toward Rosings Park and was soon out of sight.

Elizabeth hastily opened the missive and read:

Be not alarmed, Madam on receiving this letter, by the apprehension of it containing any repetition of those sentiments, or renewal of those offers which were last night so disgusting to you.

She flushed, realizing how angry and judgmental she must have appeared.

I write without any intention of paining you, but felt that my character required this to be written.

First, I apologize for any suffering I caused your sister. I realize now that when I observed her at the Netherfield Ball, she was not well, and I was unable to judge accurately her feelings for Mr. Bingley. To the extent that I misunderstood the depths of her regard, I apologize. I also realize that I overstepped the bounds of my friendship with Bingley by advising him so strongly. Although it is too late to make amends, I will say that Bingley appeared to have a sincere admiration for your sister. Whether that would ultimately have grown into a lasting passion, I do not know. I am no expert in that emotion, having only recently felt its devastating effects myself.

Did that mean that Mr. Darcy had not felt a passion for his wife? And that he now felt a lasting passion for her?

She felt the blood rush to her face, then returned to the letter.

But suffice it to say that I am sorry that your sister's last days were sorrowful, and I wish that I could turn back time and act differently.

Elizabeth held the letter against her bosom for a

few moments, overwhelmed by the feelings his words inspired.

She sensed that he was honest and that he truly apologized for his actions. She spent a few minutes thinking of Jane and how different her life might have been if Bingley had returned to Netherfield. Would Jane have recovered her health? Would she have lived to marry Mr. Bingley? Elizabeth did not know, and could never know, but Mr. Darcy's words helped in a small measure to alleviate some of her pain. She wished that there was a way for Jane to know that Mr. Bingley had cared for her. But perhaps she knew already from her vantage point in heaven.

And knowing Jane, she had already forgiven everyone involved. She had nothing bad to say about Bingley while living and she would have forgiven Mr. Darcy as well.

Elizabeth returned to the letter.

As for your defence of Mr. Wickham, I appeal to your sense of justice. I am not the only one who knows the facts of his dealings with my family. You may speak to Colonel Fitzwilliam, if you wish to know more. He knows of my father's will and the payment Wickham received. He also knows that Anne never loved Wickham. The Colonel was a frequent visitor at Pemberley and Rosings Park as we all grew up together.

He knows as well as I that Wickham treated Anne abominably, teasing her and mocking her poor health. She thoroughly disliked him and in later years, refused to speak to him. I don't know what story he told you or his motivation, but once again, I am forced to tell you that it is a lie.

Could this be true? Elizabeth searched her memory, trying to recall Wickham and his face as he had told her about Anne de Bourgh. He had first asked if Mr. Darcy had given her any specifics when he said that he was not to be trusted with women.

When she said that she had no further details, had he thought he could concoct a tale and that she would believe it?

And there is one other matter that I had hoped to tell no one, but feel that I must disclose to you now. You have met my sister Georgiana. When my father died five years ago, Colonel Fitzwilliam and I became her guardians. Last year she was in Ramsgate for the summer under the supervision of a woman named Mrs. Younge. Unbeknownst to us, Mrs. Younge was a prior acquaintance of Mr. Wickham. Together they contrived, and Mr. Wickham managed to convince my sister that she loved him and to agree to an elopement. She was but then only fifteen, which must be her excuse. Fortunately I joined them unexpectedly, a day or two before the intended elopement and Georgiana told me all. You may imagine what I felt and how I acted. Mr. Wickham's chief object was unquestionably my sister's fortune, which is thirty thousand pounds; but I cannot help supposing that the hope of revenging himself on me was a strong inducement. For the truth of this matter, you may speak to Colonel Fitzwilliam or my sister who gave me permission to tell you.

Wickham had tried to elope with Miss Darcy?

Now Elizabeth did not know what to think. She knew Mr. Wickham had proposed to Miss King once she was an heiress. Could he have targeted Miss Darcy as well? Miss Darcy was a sweet, painfully shy girl, who rarely said anything in public. She understood how Miss Darcy would have been overwhelmed by his attentions.

Although Mr. Darcy had said she could ask the Colonel or his sister, she knew she would not. He would not have given his permission unless he knew they would corroborate his words, and she could not bring herself to ask them and to embarrass them both.

She thought now of Mr. Wickham's words at Jane's funeral. What had been his motives? Had he been trying to take advantage of her grief by suggesting that they meet clandestinely?

What did she know of his trustworthiness other than his charming manner?

Elizabeth felt ashamed. She had always prided herself on her discernment and now it appeared that she had trusted the wrong man. She had distrusted Darcy because he disparaged her looks and had the strength of mind to disagree with her. Whereas Wickham had deceived her by his flattering attentions. She realized now how inconsistent Wickham had been in his stories. First Darcy had hated him because his father preferred him, and then Darcy had hated him because his wife loved him. How convenient for Wickham that both those individuals were safely dead and could not speak for themselves.

She saw now the impropriety and the indelicacy of his putting himself forward as he had done when they first met.

Mr. Darcy had tried to warn her at the Netherfield Ball, and she had been too proud to listen to him.

She had been blind and foolish. She looked back at the letter.

Last of all, I must address your concerns about my daughter Juliette. Perhaps I was harsh the day you found her by the stream. In my defence, I may be overly fearful for her safety. One of my younger brothers died in a drowning accident. He had gone off by himself, not telling anyone where he was going. To this day, I wish that I had been at home and that I had been able to prevent the accident.

Elizabeth did not know what to think. Her heart ached to think of Darcy's loss, and now she understood his fears for Juliette. She continued reading.

My parents loved me, but they were not affectionate or demonstrative. I admired the way you were able to speak to my daughter and your suggestions for her care and education. You appear to have had a loving relationship with your own father. In asking you to marry me, I hoped that you would help me create a greater bond with my own child and one day be the mother of my future children. I want them to have a mother who will love them and laugh with them.

But since you have refused me, I will look elsewhere. I will only add, God bless you.

Fitzwilliam Darcy

Elizabeth sighed at the kindness of his closing and promptly read the letter again.

* * *

Darcy, Fitzwilliam and the rest of their party prepared to leave Rosings that morning. Mr. Darcy and the Colonel paid one last visit to the parsonage.

Darcy did not know if he would see Elizabeth again, but hoped he would. He wondered if his letter had made any impression upon him at all, or if she still despised him.

Elizabeth came into the room as he was speaking with Mrs. Collins. "Mr. Darcy," she said coolly. "Are you leaving today?"

Her beautiful face was inscrutable. He said, "Yes."

"Then, if you will permit me, I will provide you a list of the books I mentioned the other day."

"I would appreciate it, thank you."

She handed him an envelope. "Here it is."

He saw that neither Mrs. Collins nor her husband took any notice of the event. "Thank you, Miss Bennet," he said formally.

"You are most welcome."

His gaze sought hers and he saw that her checks were slightly pink.

After a few more minutes they all said their farewells and left. He looked back at Elizabeth one last time, looking at the woman that he loved so desperately. He had thought that she was expecting his addresses, that she had been flirting with him, but all that time she had hated him.

In the carriage, Georgiana said, "I like Miss Bennet."

The Colonel looked meaningfully at Darcy. "So do I."

Mr. Darcy said nothing.

"Aren't you going to read her letter?" Georgiana asked.

"It is a list of books," Darcy corrected. "I will read it later."

The Colonel purposefully changed the subject, earning his gratitude.

Later that night Darcy opened her missive when he was alone. He admired her even handwriting. There was a list of books on the first page, and on the second, a brief message to him.

I accept your apology and offer mine. I have misjudged you. The matter you referenced yesterday I agree is best forgotten, although I do wish you success elsewhere.

Darcy wondered how long it had taken for her to write what would be understood only by him. He admired her caution in leaving no salutation, no signature to link the statements back to her.

He read the words several times, marvelling at the warmth that filled his breast. *I have misjudged you.* She did not hate him. His letter had made a difference.

And although she still did not want his proposal, he now had hope.

* * *

Mr. Bennet came out of his library and greeted Elizabeth when she finally returned home. He smiled. "I have missed you greatly, Lizzy. More than you can imagine. I am afraid I assuaged my grief by being overly extravagant at the booksellers." His eyes sparkled. "But oh, what fun we will have reading and discussing them together."

When she saw him, Elizabeth realized how much she had missed him as well. With Jane gone, he was now her favourite family member – the one who knew her best.

She dutifully looked through the stack of new books, admiring the titles. She would enjoy reading them with her father, and not only for the intellectual occupation. She needed something to keep herself from thinking about Mr. Darcy and his unsettling proposal.

As much as she would like to confide in someone, she would not tell her father, for he might turn it into a joke and tease her.

And now that she knew Mr. Darcy better, she did not want to make fun of him. She regretted all the foolish things she had said about him before.

"How are the Collinses?" her father asked. "And you must tell me about Lady Catherine de Bourgh.

Did she live up to her reputation?"

"She is an opinionated, wealthy woman, accustomed to getting her own way," Elizabeth said. "But I can pity her, for she is still grieving the death of her daughter, Mr. Darcy's wife."

Mr. Bennet looked disappointed. "If I did not know better, I would think I was speaking to Jane. Where has my clever Lizzy gone?"

Clever Lizzy had been humbled by Mr. Darcy. She saw now how quick she had been to judge others and find fault. "We should all become more like Jane," she said quietly.

"Perhaps so," he admitted. "But I don't want you to lose your sense of humour."

"I don't want to lose it either, but perhaps I will regulate it more closely."

"You do as you think best," he said finally. "You are a good girl."

Upon rejoining the rest of her family, Elizabeth was surprised to learn that Lydia was not at home. She had gone to Brighton with Mrs. Forster, Captain Forster's wife. The militia had moved to Brighton. So that meant Mr. Wickham was gone as well. Elizabeth was not sad to hear that. She had worried, wondering what she would say when she saw him again.

Kitty said, "And you'll never guess what has

happened to Wickham."

Her eyes widened. Had his villainy been discovered?

"He is no longer engaged to Miss King. He is free once more."

Elizabeth was doubly glad that he was gone, then. Not that he would have ever bothered her. Without a dowry, she was too poor to tempt him to marriage, but she was relieved that she would not have to speak to him again. "I hope Miss King isn't heartbroken," she said kindly.

"Oh, I am certain she will find someone else with her fortune. If I had a fortune, I would be married by now. It's so unfair."

Elizabeth asked, "But would you want to marry a man who was only marrying you for your money?"

Kitty looked at her with incomprehension and Mrs. Bennet joined the conversation. "I agree. Life is unfair. But when a young woman does not have a large dowry, she must emphasize other assets. Men are simple creatures. They like a pretty face and a well-turned ankle. Never underestimate the power of a smile and a compliment. You would do well to take Lydia as a model, Kitty. If you are not careful, she will be married before you."

Kitty pouted. "But there is no one here in

Meryton. All the officers are in Brighton." She wailed, "I'm going to end up an old maid like Elizabeth."

"Kitty, that's unkind," Mrs. Bennet said sharply. "I'm certain Elizabeth has done her best. It is not her fault she couldn't bring Mr. Collins up to scratch." She turned to Elizabeth. "I suppose there weren't any eligible young men in Hunsford?"

She thought of Mr. Darcy and wondered what her stepmother would say if she knew she had refused a man with ten thousand pounds a year. She would probably think it was time to have her committed at Bedlam. "No one who was eligible," she said finally.

* * *

Once he had returned to Pemberley, Darcy wrote to Bingley, telling him of Jane Bennet's death. He offered to accompany him to Netherfield if he was planning to close the house. He hoped Bingley would take his suggestion. Otherwise it would be difficult to engineer a reason to return to Meryton and see Elizabeth again.

* * *

Within days Elizabeth's life fell into a steady, if boring, pattern. She woke, went walking before breakfast and then ate with her sisters. In mid-morning she often read with her father, then there was luncheon and the possibility of walking into town or going to visit one of their neighbours. Evenings were dull, with little more than the possibility of music or cards, unless they dined with Mrs. Phillips or one of their friends. And even then, the conversations seemed repetitive and inconsequential.

Elizabeth missed Jane terribly. She began to think that even Hunsford with the annoyances of Mr. Collins and Lady Catherine were more interesting than Longbourn.

A week later, Elizabeth was woken by Hill. "Oh, Miss Elizabeth, you must wake. Your father is dead and I will have to tell your stepmother."

Elizabeth blinked, unable to comprehend. "Dead? Are you certain?" She hastily wrapped a shawl around herself and followed Hill into the library.

"I thought at first he had fallen asleep reading as he sometimes does," Hill said. "I came in to light the fire, but he didn't stir."

Elizabeth walked over to her father, who sat in one of his favourite chairs, slumped down. His glasses had fallen to the floor. She touched his forehead. It was cold to the touch.

Dead without warning. Unlike Jane, he hadn't been ill, so perhaps it was his heart. But the cause of his death did not matter now. At least his face was peaceful, which made her hope that death had been quick and painless.

"We must tell Mrs. Bennet," the older woman reminded.

Elizabeth could tell that Hill did not want to be the one to do it. "I will do it."

Slowly she walked back upstairs to her parent's bedroom. She hesitated, hating to spread the bad news, but knowing that there was no changing it. First Jane and now her father. She hoped that the shock would not kill her stepmother.

But Mrs. Bennet's reaction was completely unexpected. Rather than cry and wail, she sat perfectly still for several minutes, as if shocked.

"Do you think she heard you?" Mrs. Hill asked quietly from the hallway.

"Dear me," Mrs. Bennet said finally. "I was afraid this would happen, and now it has. Mr. Bennet gone. Poor man. I always knew books would be the death of him. And what is to happen to us?" She sighed. "If only Jane had lived and married Mr. Bingley, everything would be better. Or if you had married Mr. Collins, Lizzy."

Elizabeth flinched.

Her stepmother continued. "And now to think that the conniving Charlotte Lucas is going to be mistress of my house. Well," Mrs. Bennet said with vigour, "She is not going to kick us out. We will leave immediately after the funeral. I suppose the first thing to do is order black gowns and start a reducing diet."

Elizabeth was startled by her words. "A reducing diet?"

"Yes, for I refuse to be a fat widow. It is bad enough that I will have to wear black with my complexion, but if I lose a stone, I will look much more elegant. I shall have to see if some of my better gowns can be dyed."

"What about the funeral?"

"You and Pastor Michaels can take care of that," Mrs. Bennet said.

Elizabeth supposed that made sense. She had arranged Jane's funeral. "And where are we to live?"

"My brother Edward will take us in."

Elizabeth thought of the Gardiner's house in Cheapside. It was lovely, but it would be crowded with an additional five inhabitants. "Would you like me to write to Lydia and arrange for her to come home? We must write quickly or she will not have time to travel and arrive before the funeral."

"Absolutely not," Mrs. Bennet said decisively. "She must remain in Brighton."

Elizabeth said, "But surely out of respect for her father . . ."

"No. Lydia needs to stay exactly where she is," Mrs. Bennet said decisively. "The time for sentiment is over. She is much more likely to get a husband in Brighton than here in Meryton or in London where we know no one."

"Is that all you care about?" Elizabeth said sharply, then regretted the impulse. "Forgive me, I know this is a difficult time."

Mrs. Bennet was not offended. She said, "I have to be practical, Lizzy, and plan for the future. With Mr. Bennet gone, I have to rely on myself and not waste my limited resources. It could be expensive to bring Lydia home, and if she came home, she couldn't go back. It is better that she stay with Colonel Forster."

"What if the news of Mr. Bennet's death reaches Brighton?"

"I doubt it will, but I'll write to Lydia and tell her so she will be prepared, in case it does."

Elizabeth looked at the woman who had been her mother in amazement. She felt as if she had never known her. Here her father wasn't even cold in his grave and all she could think of was money and how to get her daughters married? Had she never loved her husband? "I will go talk to the parson," she said quietly.

The next few weeks were distressing and terrible, but Elizabeth found she could bear it for she felt as if her heart was frozen. After Jane's death she thought she would never stop crying, but with her father's death, there were no tears left. She dutifully arranged the funeral and helped with the moving arrangements, feeling nothing.

She said little and ate little.

The Gardiners welcomed them in Cheapside, but the living arrangements were crowded and uncomfortable. Elizabeth had to share a room with both Mary and Kitty, but she did not mind. What did her sleeping arrangements matter? What did anything matter? She woke, ate, and went about the obligations of her day, caring for nothing.

Mrs. Gardiner was concerned and spoke to her husband privately one morning before they left their bedroom. "What can we do for poor Lizzy? Nothing interests her. She does not read; she does not play the pianoforte. I fear that she will sink further into a decline and follow her father to the grave."

"No one dies of a broken heart," Mr. Gardiner said reasonably

"I am not so certain of that. What can we do to make her happier?"

"I can take her to the booksellers," Mr. Gardiner offered. "Hopefully that will peak her interest."

Mrs. Gardiner gave her husband a quick kiss. "Excellent notion. I knew I could count on your assistance."

CHAPTER NINE

A few days later Elizabeth accompanied Mr. Gardiner to a bookseller's shop. Their intent was to sell the remainder of Mr. Bennet's library. Elizabeth was to choose out a dozen for herself, and the rest were to be sold per Mrs. Bennet's instructions. Together they rode in a hackney carriage with a manservant to do the heavy lifting. Elizabeth was glad to be going somewhere, anywhere different to escape the monotony of her new home.

"The store is not in a fashionable part of town," Mr. Gardiner warned. "Your father discovered it when he was a young man, and he recommended the place to me after he married my sister. I have found it to be a treasure trove." Mr. Gardiner was in the furnishings business and often had need to buy or sell books as well. "I think it is fitting to sell the majority of your father's books back to the place where he first bought them."

"Books like homing pigeons?" Elizabeth said lightly, and Mr. Gardiner smiled in return.

"Precisely."

The outside of the store was not promising. Although clean, the door and trim needed paint. The store had a large front window displaying books. Inside there were comfortable chairs and a table where customers could sit and read. Beyond a front counter there were rooms filled with shelves and wooden boxes. The air inside was dusty and reminded Elizabeth of her father's library. For a moment she closed her eyes and breathed in the familiar smell of old books.

The owner of the establishment was a small, white haired man with a neat waistcoat and jacket. "Good day, Mr. Gardiner," he said happily. "What is it today – buying or selling?"

"Selling," Mr. Gardiner said. "And we must go through every volume for my niece is going to reserve a few for herself."

"I don't wish to be a bother," Elizabeth said.

"No bother at all," the owner said. "Take as much time as you need. Books can be like children; we don't want to let them go."

It was a daunting task to look at all of her father's

books and choose only a few for herself. She knew his favourites well, but she could not keep all of them. The Gardiner's home was not large enough to house them, and her stepmother wanted them sold. Not surprisingly, she preferred money to knowledge.

Elizabeth sat down at a table and began going through the first box, taking out each volume and considering it before deciding whether she should keep it or let it go to someone else.

As she worked, an elderly servant woman approached her. "Excuse me, miss. Pardon me for staring, but for a moment I felt as if I had seen a ghost." She turned to the owner. "She reminds me of Ginny, the girl from the Blue Pheasant."

The owner smiled. "Yes, she does have the look of her."

"The Blue Pheasant?" Elizabeth said, intrigued. "By any chance are you referring to Virginia Caldwell?"

The woman beamed. "Yes, I believe that was her name. Do you know the woman?"

"I am her daughter."

The old woman clapped her hands together. "Heavens. I wondered what had become of her. So she married. Good for her. Is she well, is she still living?"

Elizabeth shook her head. "No, she died when I was born."

"I am sorry to hear that. She was a lovely young woman, always reading." She curtsied. "But I'll let you get back to your reading, too, Miss."

Within two hours Mr. Gardiner had negotiated the sale, and a box of books was packed for them to take home. As they left the store, Mr. Gardiner asked Elizabeth if she would like to see the Blue Pheasant. "I have obtained directions. I don't know if it is still owned by your mother's family, but we can ask."

"I would like that, thank you," Elizabeth said. She would like to see where her mother had lived.

As the hackney coach drove them to the location, the streets became darker, more narrow. Mr. Gardiner appeared concerned. "Perhaps this was not a good idea," he said as the coach stopped before an ill-kept establishment with dirty windows. "This looks more like a boarding house with a pub rather than a proper inn."

"Surely we won't come to harm by merely stepping inside for five minutes," Elizabeth said, still intrigued.

"If you wish," Mr. Gardner said and accompanied her. "But five minutes only, mind. We will not be dining." He ordered the hackney to wait for them and told his manservant, "Stay close."

As the stepped through the door, they were approached by a large, ill-kempt man with greasy hair pulled back with a black ribbon. His shirt was yellowed and frayed along the neck. "How can I help you sir?" He looked them both up and down, noting the difference in their ages. "Will you be wanting a room? I can charge by the hour."

Mr. Gardiner was offended. "Indeed not."

Elizabeth put her hand on his arm. "Uncle Gardiner," she said quietly, "We don't need to stay."

"There is no point in coming unless we learn something," Mr. Gardiner said quietly. "For all we know, he is one of the employees." He turned to the man. "Excuse me, I am looking for Mr. Caldwell. I believe he is the owner of this establishment."

"I'm Caldwell."

Elizabeth flinched. This could not be her grandfather. He was most likely an uncle or a cousin. She lifted her chin. She said, "I am Elizabeth Bennet, Virginia Caldwell's daughter."

The man peered at her. "You have the look of her. What do you want?"

"Nothing, sir," Mr. Gardiner said sharply. "We were merely in the area and thought to pay our respects."

The man spoke to Elizabeth. "Do you want money? You thinking that with your grandfather's death maybe you should inherit something?"

She shrank back, "No."

"Good, because there wasn't nothing to inherit."

"That will be enough," Mr. Gardiner said to Elizabeth and took her arm. "Good day, sir."

Once they were back in the carriage, Elizabeth apologized. "You were right, Uncle. We should not have gone inside."

"It wasn't so very bad," Mr. Gardiner said, trying to be positive. "No doubt the place was better when your grandfather owned it. The current owner doesn't seem to know how to run a business."

Elizabeth said nothing. She realized that her father had painted a rosier picture of her mother than the truth. She was not the granddaughter of a prosperous innkeeper after all. She was the niece of that vulgar, dirty man. She shivered. She glanced briefly at Mr. Gardiner, who in actuality was not her uncle, merely the brother of her stepmother. She realized now that with her father's death, she was an orphan. And her closest blood relations consisted of Mr. Collins and that man at the Blue Pheasant. It was a lowering thought.

Later that evening Mr. Gardiner reported on the

visit to his wife when they were abed. She sighed. "That is too bad. I had hoped the day would be a pleasant one."

"It had its pleasant moments," Mr. Gardiner said.

Mrs. Gardiner smiled. "That's one of the reasons why I love you, sir. You never let yourself get discouraged."

"Perhaps there is something else we can do for Lizzy."

"I will think on it."

"But not right now," Mr. Gardiner said and kissed her.

Mrs. Gardiner sighed and smiled wide. She wrapped her arms around him. "No, not right now."

* * *

Georgiana spoke. "Brother, I believe that is Miss Bennet."

Darcy's heart leapt at the words. Elizabeth here, in London? He had imagined her safely back at Longbourn. He turned and looked across the art gallery floor and saw a young woman, dressed in black. Her face was half hidden by a poke bonnet, but as she turned to address a woman standing next to her and he saw that it was she. She looked thinner.

For a moment he was concerned for her health.

He left Georgiana with Mrs. Annesley and walked rapidly towards her. He did not want to miss the opportunity to speak with her. "Miss Bennet," he said cheerfully. "What a pleasure to see you."

She startled as she recognized him. "Sir."

"Are you well?"

"Yes, thank you."

"And your family?"

She looked disconcerted. "Well enough," she said finally.

He frowned at her tone and she explained, "My family now resides in London. My father recently died."

His heart contracted with sympathy. He well remembered the death of each of his parents. "I am sorry to hear that. Had he been ill?"

"No, it was quite a shock."

"And the Collinses have inherited." The moment the words were out of his mouth, he felt stupid for reminding her of her misfortunes.

"Yes."

"Then Meryton's loss is London's gain. I hope you are enjoying your stay here."

"Very much, thank you." She said, "And you, sir are you and your family well?"

He was glad that she cared enough to ask. "Yes, I

am in Town with Georgiana for a few days. I had business to conduct and she wanted to shop." He smiled. "Juliette is at Pemberley."

He saw the other members of her party – a fashionable, well-dressed couple who stood back. They seemed interested in their conversation but were too polite to interfere. "Would you do me the honour of introducing me to your friends?"

She seemed surprised that he would ask, but the introduction was immediately made. Mr. Darcy learned that they were her aunt and uncle. Her uncle Mr. Edward Gardiner was brother to her stepmother. They spoke for a few minutes about the art exhibit and the weather. Mr. Darcy also discovered that Mr. Gardiner owned a business acquiring and selling furnishings. "I believe I have been in your shop," Mr. Darcy said when he learned its location. "I remember purchasing a little Italian mirror for my sister's bedchamber."

Mr. Gardiner nodded, pleased.

In the course of the conversation, he also learned that Mrs. Gardiner had spent much of her younger years in Lambton, a small town five miles from Pemberley. Mrs. Gardiner spoke kindly of his parents. "Your father was one of the best of men," she said.

"Thank you," Darcy said. He hoped that one day people would say the same of him.

The conversation shifted to the art before them, and they all admired a pastoral scene. Mr. Gardiner said something about the location looking ideal for fishing.

"Do you enjoy fishing, sir?"

"Yes, but I rarely get the opportunity."

'Perhaps someday you would care to visit my home. Perhaps the next time you visit Lambton with your wife. I would be pleased to provide you whatever tackle you need and I could point out those parts of the stream where there is usually most sport."

"You are most kind, sir. Perhaps one day I will take you up on the offer."

"Do," Darcy said and saw that Elizabeth eyes widened at his invitation. For a moment, he wished yet again that she had accepted his proposal, and then his conversations with her extended family would be more natural.

Elizabeth watched their interaction with composure but added little to the conversation. She seemed unnaturally subdued. He wished he knew what she thought of him, if she wished to further the acquaintance or to avoid him completely. She said little, seeming content to let him and her relations converse.

After a few minutes, his sister Georgiana approached with Miss Annesley beside her, and he asked Elizabeth permission to introduce her to her family as well. Georgiana was pleased to learn that Mrs. Gardiner had lived in Lampton and they tried to determine if they knew anyone in common, but eventually the conversation lagged. Darcy tried to think of something more to say to prolong the visit.

"Mrs. Gardiner, I have a favour to ask, if I may."

She smiled. "Yes, sir?"

"By any chance, do you employ a governess?"

"Yes."

"Then perhaps you could give me some advice. Recently, it was suggested that I employ a governess for my daughter who is four years old." He glanced briefly at Elizabeth, who smiled at him. He turned back to her aunt. "Can you recommend where I could find such a woman?"

Mrs. Gardiner smiled, pleased by the request. "I believe that personal references are best. We obtained our governess Miss Barnes after she had been employed by a friend. However, we have often used Broadmoor Employment Services to obtain other servants and I believe they arrange for governesses as well as household staff."

"Where are they located?"

Mrs. Gardiner provided the address. Darcy thanked her and after conversing for a few more minutes, properly took his leave.

* * *

Mrs. Gardiner waited until they were in the hackney cab, riding home, to mention Mr. Darcy. "Elizabeth," she teased. "I did not realize you knew Mr. Darcy so well."

Elizabeth flushed. "Do you like him?"

Mr. Gardiner said, "He appears to be a superior gentleman. He is perfectly well behaved, polite and unassuming."

Mrs. Gardiner said, "There is something a little stately in him, but I would not call him proud. In fact, I do not find him disagreeable at all"

Elizabeth regretted her prior descriptions of the man. "No, I believe I was mistaken before. His manners are excellent."

"From what we have seen of him," Mrs. Gardiner continued, "I find it difficult to believe that he could have behaved in such a cruel a way to Mr. Wickham."

Elizabeth was surprised by the reference, then remembered that her aunt knew of Wickham. Back at Christmas time, Lydia had shared all of Wickham's melodramatic history with her aunt.

Elizabeth bit her lip, thinking of what she knew but could not disclose. "I don't think we know all the particulars in that matter, aunt. I have heard that Mr. Wickham was actually paid to relinquish his legal claims."

"So your Mr. Darcy is not such a villain?"

Elizabeth said quickly, "Not my Mr. Darcy."

"I beg to differ," Mrs. Gardiner said. "I saw the look on his face when he saw you. I believe he cares for you."

Elizabeth did not know what to say. She believed that his attentions today had merely been politeness, nothing more.

"And you my dear, appeared to be at a loss for words. I have never seen you so flustered. But forgive me, I will not be like your stepmother and tease you. Time will prove whether he cares for you or not."

Elizabeth appreciated the silence. She looked out the carriage window rather than meeting her aunt's inquiring gaze. Did Mr. Darcy still care for her? She was amazed by his civility. Never in her life had she seen his manners so little dignified, never had he spoken with such gentleness. He had honoured her relations, even going so far as to invite Mr. Gardiner to Pemberley.

What could it mean? Had he truly changed or had she merely learned to understand and respect him?

When they returned to Gracechurch Street, she was met by her stepmother who had declined the trip to the art gallery. "What do you think of my hair, Lizzy?" Mrs. Bennet cried happily, turning about so she could admire it.

Elizabeth blinked in astonishment. Her stepmother's hair, which had always been fair, was now almost white but with a faint orange tint. "Is this a new fashion?" she asked, afraid of the answer.

"Madame Colette says it takes ten years off my age."

Elizabeth did not know what to say, but Mrs. Bennet did not notice. She was too busy talking, discussing her plans to go shopping the next day where she might be seen. She giggled with Kitty about the possibility of their being mistaken for sisters. Mary was disgusted by the conversation and left to read in her room.

"Don't blame me if you turn out to be an old maid," Mrs. Bennet called after her. Then she turned on Elizabeth, surveying her critically. "Perhaps you should have your hair done as well, Lizzy. You need to do something. You are too thin now and pale. If you are not careful, you will look haggard."

"Thank you for your concern," Elizabeth said. "But for the present I will keep my hair as God made it."

"As you wish," Mrs. Bennet said airily. "But remember, you are not growing any younger."

"Yes, ma'am."

The next day Elizabeth spoke to her Aunt Gardiner, expressing her concerns. "I don't think I can bear to accompany my stepmother out in public. She looks like a fright."

"Do not worry, Lizzy," Mrs. Gardiner said kindly. "Wherever you are known, you will be respected and valued. You will not appear to less advantage for having a —" she hesitated. "a silly stepmother."

Elizabeth knew she meant well, but it did not make her feel better.

"The right man will not mind."

She supposed her aunt was referring to Mr. Darcy. In actuality, he had not minded. When they were in Rosings, his feelings for her had been so strong, they had overcome his scruples. But she felt that if he saw her stepmother now with her atrocious hair, he would count his blessings that she had rejected him.

That night Elizabeth grew increasingly restless. She was not happy in Gracechurch. She did not want to spend time socializing with her stepmother, and she was not needed by Mrs. Gardiner. She felt as if she had no purpose and that she was a burden to her family.

Both her stepmother and her aunt thought she should marry, but Elizabeth knew that was not the answer. She had no desire to marry at present. Her heart was too troubled over the death of Jane and her father. She felt as if she had no love to give, and she would not marry without love. She stared at the ceiling and sighed. There must be something else she could do.

Two days after the trip to the art gallery, Elizabeth decided to take a hackney carriage to the employment agency. Perhaps she could be a governess or a paid companion. She slipped out in the afternoon without telling anyone. If she was going to become independent, she could not rely on others. Besides, she was afraid that if she told her aunt, she would be forbidden to go.

As she left the carriage and walked towards the front door of the agency, she saw a tall gentleman leave the building. It was Mr. Darcy. He appeared stunned to see her. "Miss Bennet?"

She hesitated. At first she thought it was a coincidence, then she remembered that he also knew of the employment agency from her aunt. "Good day, sir. Have you found a governess for your daughter?"

"I have begun the process. No doubt I will interview some applicants later this week."

"Very good. I hope you find someone suitable."

"And you, are you looking for a governess as well?"

Elizabeth flushed. There was no hiding it. If she was going to find work for herself, she must get over her fears of what other people would think. She lifted her chin. "Actually, I am going to apply for a position."

He was stunned. "You? But why?"

"I do not enjoy London or the social arena. My aunt's house is crowded and I feel like I am a burden on her and my stepmother. I would rather be gone and earn my living."

"But when there is no financial need –"

She said, "You don't understand."

"No, I don't. For a gentleman's daughter should not be reduced to such circumstances."

"It is my own choice."

He stood for a moment, mentally struggling to find the appropriate words. "Miss Bennet, forgive my impertinence. You are a grown woman, naturally you may choose your course in life, but this does not seem wise. Would it not be better to marry than to work as a servant?"

For a moment, Elizabeth's ironic sense of humour was tickled. She never thought that Mr. Darcy and her stepmother would have something in common. They both thought she should marry. "Governesses are not exactly servants," she said finally. "Besides, there is no one for me to marry."

His eyes seemed to burn into hers. "My offer still stands."

She felt her face flush with embarrassment. She hoped he didn't think she was begging for a proposal. She should never have told him what she was doing. "You are generous sir, but I fear you are offering out of pity."

"No, my thoughts and wishes are as they were in Hunsford.

She thought it was amazing that he would lower himself once again, offering to marry her a second time. He must still think he loved her. But would he love her when he observed her stepmother close at hand? And what of her relations from the Blue Pheasant? If she married him, it was likely that they would all dun him. His family and friends would justifiably be appalled by his choice.

For a moment Elizabeth was tempted. She did not love Mr. Darcy; she felt nothing for him but admiration now. But that was madness. She could not allow him to lower himself. "I appreciate the offer sir, but –"

"You still despise me?"

"No, not that," she said quickly. "It is just that I have too much respect and admiration for you to let you marry a woman who does not love you. You deserve better."

"Should I not be the judge of that? I believe if we married that love and affection would grow."

And if it did not? She did not want to trap him into a marriage as her stepmother had trapped her father. The words seemed to choke in her throat. "I am sorry, I must decline."

Mr. Darcy stood for a moment as if debating what he should say. "If you will not be my wife, would you consider becoming Juliette's governess?"

"No, that would be too embarrassing. You would not want that, not after your proposals."

He stiffened as if she had insulted him. "I promise you that if you were in my employ, I would never reference my proposals. You should have no fear that I would overstep the bounds of propriety. I offer you the position freely, with no ulterior motives."

He was a good man, but she could not take his offer seriously. "No sir, I appreciate your kindness, but I cannot accept."

"If you insist."

From the coolness of his tone, she knew she had offended him. She had hurt his feelings, and yet she did not know what else she could say and remain true to her own. "I do insist," she said. "And now, I would say good day to you, sir. I must go inside."

He held the door open for her.

CHAPTER TEN

Darcy watched as the employment agency door shut behind Elizabeth. He could not believe it. Miss Bennet had spoken. She did not love him, and she was not even willing to become his governess. She would rather work for a stranger.

She had tried to be polite, but she truly wanted nothing to do with him. When she spoke to him, her voice was flat with no emotion. The light hearted girl he had fallen in love with was gone. She did not tease or flirt with him. She did not even hate him. She felt absolutely nothing for him.

His future seemed bleak.

He waited outside the agency until she left the building. "Mr. Darcy," she said coolly. "Is there a problem?"

"No, I decided to wait for you, to give you a ride back to the Gardiners."

"That is not necessary."

"Perhaps not. But if you are determined to support yourself, at least I can save you the cost of a fare."

She nodded. "Thank you."

They rode in silence, both of them deep in their private thoughts. As they neared her residence, she asked to be let down at the end of the street. "I don't want to give rise to any talk."

"That is wise." He signalled for his driver to stop. He helped Miss Bennet down onto the street. He held her gloved hand for a moment and did not want to let it go.

"Thank you, sir."

"Good day, Miss Bennet. I do not agree with your decisions at present, but I wish you safety and happiness."

* * *

Darcy truly is a good man, Elizabeth thought as she said good-bye. She was still amazed that she had ever believed Wickham's lies.

Later in the privacy of her room, she removed her bonnet and pelisse and thought of her interview with the employment agent. He had taken down her name and direction but had not been encouraging. "I don't know many will want to hire you without any experience or letters of reference, Miss."

"But how am I to get experience if no one is willing to hire me?"

He did not have an answer to that.

Elizabeth did not want to ask her aunt or uncle for a letter, so she thought of Miss Barnes, their governess. If she could not provide a letter, she might be able to suggest someone who could.

She found Miss Barnes in the nursery, busy folding the children's clothes. The children were currently with Mrs. Gardiner. Miss Barnes was a tall thin woman in her early forties with a calm, practical air. "Ah, Miss Bennet," she said pleasantly. "How can I help you?"

Elizabeth explained her plans, which made Miss Barnes blanche. "You cannot be serious. You don't want to become a governess."

"Why not? You seem to enjoy your work."

"Not every family is as nice as the Gardiners."

Elizabeth frowned. "What are you saying?"

"What mother is going to want to hire a young woman as pretty as you to be in her household, tempting her husband or stirring up the male servants?"

Elizabeth laughed. "I am not that pretty. Jane was

twice as pretty."

"You don't have to be pretty. Young with passable looks is dangerous enough. The wise women of character won't want to hire you, and the unscrupulous men will."

"Are you saying that men will try to seduce me?"

Miss Barnes said, "Seduce implies some sort of willingness on your part. I am saying that men will take advantage of you. With or without your consent."

Elizabeth said, "I cannot believe it. Not in a gentleman's house."

Miss Barnes shook her head at her naiveté. "Most men are stronger than we are. It is a biological fact. If you do insist on becoming a governess, I suggest you always lock your door at night and sleep with a knife under your pillow."

"A knife? Surely that is excessive."

"No. You'll wish you had one, if you do not. I wish I had."

Elizabeth could not believe what the woman was implying, "Miss Barnes, did you have trouble?"

"Yes, it was many years ago, when I was young and foolish. It was my first position. I was a governess to a young family with four children."

"And the father of the house – he –." Elizabeth

faltered. "He took liberties?"

Miss Barne's voice was matter-of-fact. "He woke me in the middle of the night, lying on top of me, removing my clothes. There was nothing I could do. He was a big man. I knew that if I screamed, we would be discovered. The next day, I turned in my resignation. The mistress of the house must have known what he had done, but she said nothing and made certain I had a good character letter."

"That is terrible," Elizabeth said.

"You needn't look so shocked. It is more common than you think. Fortunately I didn't have a child, and no one knew about it. I am only telling you because I think it should help you to be wiser and not make the mistakes I made."

"But why didn't you say something? Report him to the magistrate?"

"And ruin my own reputation? What good would that have done? Even if he had been forced to pay damages, no one afterwards would have employed me to care for their children. I would have starved or ultimately become what that man tried to make me."

"Don't tell me that the only choices for a young woman to make a living is to get married or to become a harlot."

Miss Barnes sighed. "It is the way of the world,

Miss Elizabeth. Besides, you do not have the skills to get one of the better governess positions. Your skill at the pianoforte is adequate, but not superior. You don't speak any other languages except for a smattering of French and a little Latin, which is not sought for. Your drawing skills are mediocre at best. As Miss Bennet, a gentleman's daughter, your education is passable, but as a governess yours is inferior. And what do you know of educating children?'

"Nothing much, other than the way my father taught me."

"You would do much better to stay here and let your stepmother find you a husband rather than try to get your own employment."

Elizabeth did not like what she heard, but she could not doubt Miss Barne's sincerity. She had definitely given her food for thought.

* * *

Darcy was amazed to receive a letter from Elizabeth the next day. He recognized her handwriting on the envelope. He ripped it open.

Mr. Darcy. Please forgive my forwardness in writing to you. But I have reconsidered your proposal, and if the offer is still open, I will gladly accept.

His heart seemed to beat in his throat. Were his dreams finally to be met? He wondered how soon they could wed. He would get a special license. If it would be faster, he would take her to Gretna Green.

He almost laughed at the joy of it and returned to the letter.

I would be happy to be your daughter's governess.

The words were a blow to his heart. She did not want to marry him. She would rather work for him, demeaning herself, than be his wife.

The rejection stung, even more than her first refusal. His first proposal had taken her by surprise; she had not expected it. His second proposal had also been a surprise, and she did not think it was sincere. But here, in her letter, she had had several days to consider her options and she still chose not to marry him.

His choice now was a bitter one. He could either employ her in his house or most likely never see her again. For if he did not hire her, he believed she would find another position elsewhere.

No matter how painful the prospect, he still wanted her in his life. He could not let her go, even if that meant hiring her as a governess.

He took out a piece of writing paper and began:

My Dear Miss Bennet:

* * *

Inside the letter from Mr. Darcy, there was an additional sealed letter for Mr. Gardiner. Elizabeth did not want to give it to him, but since she was living in his house, she supposed she must. Mr. Gardiner took more half an hour to read it and spoke to Mrs. Gardiner as well before summoning Elizabeth to his office and speaking to her directly. "Close the door," he told her when she had entered the room.

"Yes, sir." She stood before his desk, facing him. Her hands were clasped together in front of herself.

"Sit down. I do not mean to interrogate you."

She obeyed and waited for his response.

He picked up the letter and showed it to her. "I learn from Mr. Darcy that you intend to become a governess."

"Yes, sir."

"I know you have been unhappy after your father's death, but now I fear it is something more. Has anyone been unkind?"

"No, it is not that. You and Aunt Gardiner have been so generous. I just thought that a change of circumstances would be beneficial."

He looked at her for a few moments. "Well, Mr. Darcy outlines the terms of your employment. You will be earning twice what Miss Barnes does for only one child. He assures me that you will be safe. He seems to be an honourable man."

"He is." That was one of the reasons she had chosen to work for him. After her talk with Miss Barnes, she felt she wanted to work for a man she could trust. And she had already met his daughter Juliette and liked her.

Mr. Gardiner sighed. "Legally I have no rights to control you. If you were my own daughter I would refuse to let you go. But since you are not, I will only advise against it. Working as a governess will materially lessen your opportunities for marriage."

"There is no guarantee that I would ever marry," Elizabeth said. "Many women don't."

He nodded, accepting her argument. "So you are determined to do this."

"Yes, sir."

"Then I will not stop you. My only advice is that you promise me that you will return home to us if there is any problem. Do not think you have to stay if the position becomes unbearable."

Elizabeth sighed with relief. "I appreciate that, thank you."

Mrs. Bennet when she heard of Elizabeth's plans, thought they were foolish. "You should have married Mr. Collins when you had the chance," she said flatly. But she did not try to persuade Elizabeth to stay in London. Privately Elizabeth thought that she was happy not to have any more obligations to her. Once she was gone, her stepmother would not have to pay for her upkeep or try any longer to get her married. "Do what you think is best, my dear," Mrs. Bennet said finally. "And I hope you are happy. Mr. Darcy is a disagreeable man, to be sure, but I suppose you won't have to converse with him much. And he will have an excellent library. You will enjoy that."

Mrs. Gardiner helped her obtain several dresses suitable for her new position and gave her some advice as well. "Mr. Darcy is a young man, a single man. I don't think it is wise, Elizabeth. I know your tender heart. As you care for his daughter, you might learn to care for him as well. I don't want you to set yourself up for heartache."

"You think I will fall in love with him? I don't think there is any risk of that."

"Be wise," her aunt added. "You have known him in a different social setting, but now he will be your employer. Strictly observe the rules of your employment. Otherwise you will court disaster. Remember that you will be his servant, not his equal."

"I don't believe I have ever been his equal," she

said quietly.

Mrs. Gardiner tsked her tongue with annoyance. "Elizabeth, do not believe the foolish standards of society. You know better. You know that the worth of an individual has little to do with his rank or ancestors. It is your own individual worth that matters. And all are equal before God."

Elizabeth smiled. "You are right."

"And when I said equal, I was referring to the rules of propriety. As his employee, you will not have the freedom you enjoyed when you met at Meryton or Hunsford. You will have to guard your tongue."

Perhaps that would be better, Elizabeth thought. She regretted so much of her earlier foolishness and things she had said. "But you wish me well?"

"Yes. And I am glad you have only agreed to one year. We will be very happy when you return home to us."

Elizabeth smiled. "Who knows what will happen within a year?"

"My guess is that some of your sisters will marry. And I will have another baby."

Elizabeth's eyes opened wide. "Truly?"

"Yes." Mrs. Gardiner put a hand on her stomach. "I am surprised you haven't noticed already."

Elizabeth must have been too preoccupied with

her own sorrows. "That is wonderful," she said, but knew that another child would make the household even more crowded. It was best that she leave. "How are you? Are you well?"

Mrs. Gardiner nodded. "I am well enough. This poor babe was a bit of a surprise. Mr. Gardiner and I thought we had finished having babies." She laughed. "I feel a little like Sarah in the Bible. I think sometimes that God has a sense of humour."

Elizabeth smiled, but said nothing. It was good to know that there were happily married people in the world. Not everyone was like her father or stepmother, merely living in the same house, barely tolerating each other.

* * *

The evening after Elizabeth left for Pemberley, Mrs. Gardiner spoke to Mr. Gardiner when they were in bed together. "I am still worried about Lizzy. I don't think she should work for Mr. Darcy."

Mr. Gardiner grunted sleepily. "I don't think she will work for him long."

"Meaning?"

"Mr. Darcy is no fool. Once he has her in his house, he will try to make the arrangement permanent."

She gasped. "Do you think he will offer her a *carte blanche*?"

"No, I think he will propose to her."

"But if he wants to marry her, why hasn't he proposed by now?"

"I think he has," Mr. Gardiner said shrewdly. "I think Lizzy refused him."

"But why?"

"She isn't thinking clearly. I think she is still grieving for her father and sister."

"But you think that ultimately she will marry him."

"Yes."

"I hope you are correct. But you understand the male mind more than I."

"I give it six months," Mr. Gardiner said. "And what say you – shall it be less or more? A private wager between ourselves."

Mrs. Gardiner sighed. "I do not know and do not care, as long as he is honourable. Overall, I think it will be good for her to get out of our house. I believe it is better for her to be busy, being useful rather than moping at home."

"Don't worry," Mr. Gardiner said sleepily. "If after a year Mr. Darcy doesn't marry her, I will call him out."

* * *

Elizabeth travelled with Mr. Darcy, Miss Darcy, and Miss Annesley to Pemberley. For most of the journey, Darcy sat outside with the coachman. "My brother doesn't like to be cooped up," Miss Darcy said.

Elizabeth was glad because it gave her more time to become accustomed to her new role as governess. She decided she would take Mrs. Annesley as a guide and only speak when she was addressed directly.

As they neared Pemberley, Miss Darcy explained. "Here we are, home at last. Miss Bennet, can you see it?"

They had ridden for several minutes through lovely woods that were part of the estate. As she peered out the window, she could finally see the house. She thought Pemberley was the most beautiful house she had ever seen. It was a handsome stone building with a graceful yard. She thought of Miss Bingley's praises and felt that for once, her accolades had been justified. Elizabeth briefly thought, I could have been mistress of all this.

But no, that was foolishness. She might have been its mistress, but at what risk? Darcy would never have accepted her family. She would have ultimately brought him sorrow.

Darcy climbed down from the carriage and helped

his sister disembark. A liveried servant helped Mrs Annesley and herself. Darcy strode inside a large entryway and called for his housekeeper, Mrs. Reynolds.

Elizabeth looked around, amazed. The entryway hall was ten times the size of the largest sitting room at Longbourn. She admired a large curving staircase that led to an upper floor. The tiles beneath her feet were an elegant black and white checkerboard. Graceful classical statues flanked the entrance. Pemberley was as grand as Rosings, but decorated in a more pleasing, inviting way. "Please see that Miss Bennet is settled in her new quarters," Mr. Darcy said briskly when the housekeeper arrived, then turned to Elizabeth. "In the morning, I want to meet with you at nine to go over plans for Juliette."

How different he sounded, but she supposed that everything was different now. He was Mr. Darcy, Master of Pemberley, and she was the governess. "Yes, sir."

He nodded briefly. "Until then, Miss Bennet. I hope you will be happy here."

He was dismissing her.

Georgiana said good bye as well, and Elizabeth followed Mrs. Reynolds back down several halls until they came to her room. Mrs. Reynolds opened the door. "This will be your room."

There was a simple, neat room with a bed and a standing closet for her clothes. Next to the bed was a high backed chair and a little side table. "That is a lovely chair," Elizabeth said. "It looks very comfortable."

"It is," Mrs. Reynolds said. "It is from the Library. Mr. Darcy thought you should have a place to sit and read."

"That was very thoughtful of him."

"He is a most excellent master," Mrs. Reynolds said. "He is firm but fair and cares deeply for those in his employ. If you have any problems or difficulties, let me know."

"I will, thank you."

"I will have one of the servants bring your trunk. And will you be wanting to dine with Mrs. Annesley later this evening or have a tray in your room?"

Elizabeth said, "A tray tonight, if I may, but for most days, I will eat with everyone else. I don't want to cause extra work."

Mrs. Reynolds nodded. "Very good, ma'am. I will give you a tour of the house tomorrow morning, after you speak to the Master. And then you can meet Miss Juliette."

"I met her briefly once before, but I look forward

to getting to know her better."

"Until tomorrow, then."

Mrs. Reynolds closed the door as she left and Elizabeth sat down in the high backed chair and sighed. She was alone at last in her own room. She thought it odd that this was the first time in her life that she would not have to share a bedroom. But it felt good to be silent, with no one watching her, no one expecting anything from her.

Here at least she could be exactly as she wished. She hoped Mr. Darcy was right and that she would be happy here.

Within half an hour a footman arrived with her trunk. Elizabeth unpacked slowly and methodically, enjoying the pleasure of organizing her things within a new space. She unwrapped her present from Miss Barnes: a knife. She smiled wryly and placed it under her pillow. "Just in case, Miss Barnes," she said aloud.

* * *

Darcy sat in his office, steeling himself before Elizabeth would join him for their meeting. Having her at Pemberley was proving to be more difficult than he had imagined. During the journey he had tried to avoid her, and when he spoke to her, he strove to keep his words flat and respectful as he would to anyone else in his employ. He felt that in time, it would become easier to control his behaviour and his wayward thoughts.

But his dreams were another matter entirely. He feared that they might be his undoing.

Over the past few weeks, especially after seeing Elizabeth in London and then knowing that she would be working for him, he had tried not to think of her throughout the day, wondering what she was doing and what she was thinking or feeling. He had thought he was improving.

But then last night, he dreamt of declaring his love for her again. Instead of refusing him, she had returned his ardour, and he had woken, aching with desire.

If this continued, he did not know how he could endure her proximity.

On the other hand, making her leave would not necessarily relieve his frustration. His feelings for her seemed to be his life's blood, constantly running through his veins.

Part of him wished that he had never met her and had never fallen in love with her.

Life had been so simple with Anne. He had always known he would marry her. They admired and respected each other. Their families were connected;

their views and opinions were the same. He had cared for her deeply, had loved her in his way, but his feelings for her were nothing in comparison to the flood of emotion he felt for Elizabeth Bennet. She was mentally and physically exhilarating.

And he was her employer.

He thought of the saying that 'half a loaf is better than none.'

He should be grateful that she was in his house and that he could see her on a daily basis, even if it caused him pain.

He must learn to master his feelings.

He heard a knock on his door. "Come in," he said coolly.

Elizabeth walked in. Her beautiful hair was scraped back into a tight bun at the base of her neck and her morning dress was black, high at the neck, with no lace or decorations except for a little white collar at the neck.

"Please be seated," he said and she sat across from him, her hands neatly clasped in her lap.

She looked painfully thin. "You have eaten?" he asked, wondering what exactly the servants ate. He would have to follow up with Mrs. Reynolds to see that she was adequately fed.

"Yes, sir."

"Do you like your room?"

"Yes, sir. It is very comfortable. And thank you for the chair. Mrs. Reynolds said it was your idea."

He had wanted to share all of Pemberley with her, and now he had to be satisfied with giving her one library chair. "Good. I am glad you like it. And feel free to borrow whatever books you want from the library. You do not need to ask specifically."

She smiled. "Thank you."

Her smile was nearly his undoing. He wished they could talk naturally, without the constraints of society. But he had promised not to remind her of his desire to marry her. He cleared his throat. "Now, let us talk about Juliette. I know you had mentioned the possibility of her learning to read. I don't mind if you promote that, but I am primarily concerned with her health – that she have ample time to play outdoors and to run. Naturally, she needs to be taught manners and morals, but I believe they can be taught while she is learning other things. Her current nurse, Mrs. Sally, was my nurse as well as Georgiana's. She is a kind woman, but her health and eyesight are failing. In the past year she has not liked to go up and down stairs, so Juliette has spent too much time in the nursery. I hadn't realized what was happening until I returned from our visit to Rosings in the spring, and since then, I have endeavoured to spend more time with Juliette myself. She has started riding lessons and we often go on walks. And thanks in part to your list of books, I have been reading aloud to her whenever I am at Pemberley."

"Very good," Elizabeth said.

"I hoped you would approve."

"It is not my place to approve or disapprove."

He paused. "But I appreciate it, none the less." She looked uncomfortable, so he continued. "I must travel occasionally, and when I am gone, I want you to write to me daily, telling me of Juliette's health and progress. When I am at Pemberley, we will meet privately once a week to review her education, and one night a week you and Mrs Annesley will dine with me and Georgiana unless we have company."

"Yes, sir."

It was difficult to treat her as his employee, when all he wanted to do was to ask her what she thought of Pemberley. He said, "Do you have any questions?"

"No, sir. But I assume I will have a few as I learn the position."

He nodded. "I have no doubt that you will learn quickly. Mrs. Reynolds will give you a tour and Mrs. Sally should be a help as well."

"Yes, sir."

He wished he could think of something else to say so he could keep her longer in his office. "Very well, Miss Bennet," he said finally. "That will do."

CHAPTER ELEVEN

Pemberley was a beautiful home. It had been built originally in the 1600s and modified in the mid-1700s. Mrs. Reynolds gave her a comprehensive tour of the house. She explained that they were currently in the process of repapering and furnishing several of the guest bedrooms. Elizabeth knew that the portrait gallery would be become one of her favourite rooms, for it contained two portraits of Mr. Darcy when he was a child and one of him as a young man. There was also one portrait of his wife, the former Miss Anne de Bourgh. She was small and thin but pretty with delicate features.

The nursery was light and bright, with wide window seats. Juliette was pleased to see her. "Miss Bennet," she cried and rushed to give her a hug around her legs.

"Miss Juliette," Mrs. Sally corrected, and the little

girl pulled back. "It is good to see you again, Miss Bennet," she said properly.

"It is good to be here," Elizabeth returned.

Mrs. Sally gave her a tour of the nursery and explained a typical day, outlining the family schedule. Elizabeth was glad to find that Juliette's nurse would continue to work for Mr. Darcy, helping with Miss Juliette's clothes and watching her young charge for an hour or two every day so Miss Bennet could take a rest or do other duties. Mrs. Sally said, "I may be getting old, but I can still be useful."

Elizabeth had feared that she would see Mr. Darcy often, but the nursery seemed to be its own little world. A maid helped Miss Juliette wake, dress and supervised her breakfast. Then if the weather was fair, Juliette had riding lessons, sometimes with her father. Then she returned to the nursery for lessons and time with Miss Bennet. When Mr. Darcy was available, a servant would arrive to escort Miss Juliette downstairs to his office or one of the sitting rooms. Mr. Darcy rarely came to the nursery, and when he did, his visits were short. At those times, she withdrew to give them privacy.

She was pleased to see that he genuinely cared for his daughter. He took the time to listen to her and often hugged her. She thought of what he had said in his letter and hoped that in time, she would be able to help him be a better father.

Every day, Elizabeth felt that she was growing more comfortable with her position. It was better than living in London with her stepmother. Here she had time to think, to walk, to read. Juliette was a charming child, quick to learn. She liked writing her letters and would no doubt learn to read quickly.

Gradually, she became friends with Mrs. Annesley. Mrs. Annesley would never replace Jane, but she was a kind, pleasant woman. Elizabeth also spent some time with Miss Georgiana. Mr. Darcy's sister had sought her out. "Miss Bennet, this is so strange to have you working for us, but I am glad to see you again. I would like to play the pianoforte sometimes with you, if you are willing."

* * *

Two weeks after Elizabeth had joined the household, Darcy spoke to Mrs. Reynolds. "Tell me about Miss Bennet," he said formally. "Is she fitting in? Does she appear happy?"

"Oh, she's an excellent young woman," Mrs. Reynolds said. "Very conscientious. Quiet, but good-natured. She doesn't complain or put on airs. Mrs. Sally was worried about having a governess for Miss

Juliette when she was so young, but now she likes Miss Bennet as well."

"Very good." He was afraid to ask more for then Mrs. Reynolds might wonder at his interest. "She was very thin when she first arrived. Do you think she is well?"

"I think so. She is eating a little more, and her face has filled out. And she takes walks around the park nearly every morning."

That was interesting information. "Thank you."

He thought about her taking walks for two days before he gathered the courage to join her. He went out onto his property and waited to see her. He remembered the times he had done the same at Rosings Park. He worried that she might not come, but finally he saw her, walking along the path beside the vegetable gardens. He stepped forward to meet her. "Miss Bennet."

She startled. "Mr. Darcy. Sir."

"Do you mind if I join you?"

"No, sir."

If she were not his employee, he would have offered her his arm.

She asked, "Is there something you wish to discuss with me? Something about Juliette?"

"No. It is merely a fine day for a walk." He walked

beside her for a moment, letting her set the pace. "I see you are still an excellent walker. What do you think of Pemberley?"

"It is beautiful. I wonder at your ever wanting to leave."

He smiled, glad that she liked his home, but wished yet again that it could be her home as well.

They walked in silence for several minutes, until they came to the place where the path separated. "Miss Bennet, have you taken the opportunity to walk the longer path?"

"No, for I heard that it is nearly ten miles round."

"It is. Do you think you are not up to it?"

"I believe I do not have the time, sir."

"But Juliette will be busy with her riding lessons. We need not go all the way. We could walk a little and then turn back. The longer walk contains some of my favourite views."

She hesitated, and then agreed. "If you wish."

They did not talk again until they were beyond the view from the house. "I can see why you like it so much," Elizabeth said, looking at the groves of trees. "The grounds are beautiful here."

"They are. When I was younger, I sometimes ran around it."

"Ten miles?" she asked in amazement.

He shrugged. "I was younger, then. Wickham and I would have races, and he always won. I didn't discover until years later that he was cheating, cutting through the course."

"That seems to be his manner – to cut corners."

"Yes." But he didn't want to discuss Wickham with Elizabeth. He didn't know why he had mentioned him. He said, "I don't walk this way often enough."

"That's a shame."

"Yes, it seems foolish to own something that I don't appreciate and enjoy. No doubt there are months that go by without anyone other than an occasional gardener passing through."

"Or a poacher."

He smiled, amused as always by her clever mind. "Perhaps, but we don't seem to have much of a problem of that around here."

"You are fortunate."

In all but in love, he thought, but did not want to dwell on that. He had Elizabeth's full attention for a few minutes and he wanted to savour it. Mentioning Wickham had made him think of Georgiana. He said, "My sister has enjoyed having more of your company. She said that sometimes you practice the pianoforte together."

"Yes. She is helping me to improve my playing."

"Thank you for taking the time. I know she can be lonely. We do not have neighbours with young women her age."

Elizabeth said, "It is no hardship. She's a lovely girl."

"I would take her to London for the Season, but she doesn't like the crowds."

"She is still quite young."

"I think it would be better if she had sisters, as you do."

Elizabeth smiled at that. "Now, I know you are teasing me. You wouldn't wish her to have a sister like Lydia."

She was right, but he didn't want to offend her by agreeing, so he only smiled and they continued their stroll.

"Perhaps if Anne had lived she could have helped Georgiana," he said, thoughtfully. "But then, she was shy as well. It seems to run in the family."

"Lady Catherine is not shy."

He laughed out loud. "No. No one has ever accused her of being shy." He was reminded of his aunt's rudeness when Elizabeth visited Rosings Park. "You were not intimidated by her, though."

"No, there didn't seem to be a point in that. My

father would have found her conversation amusing, but I have sympathy for her. She misses her daughter greatly."

Darcy nodded. "I know, and I try to be patient with her as well, but sometimes it is difficult."

"I often think it is easier to have charity with strangers than with one's own family."

He thought of her stepmother. "You may be right."

As they walked, he pointed out his favourite fishing spot, which led to him asking about her uncle. "Have you heard from your family?" he asked.

"No, not yet."

"But you have written to them."

"Yes. I wrote when I first arrived, and Mrs. Reynolds arranged to have it posted."

He nodded, still amazed that she had chosen to leave her family behind to work for him.

As they walked, he stole several glances at her, admiring the clearness of her skin, her cheerful expression. Elizabeth was wearing a black dress and little leather walking boots. He thought briefly of Anne and couldn't help but make a comparison between the two women. After a few minutes, he said, "Anne never walked this path; she did not have the strength, but she did have a little pony with a cart, and when the weather was good and her health was up to it, she sometimes took a drive. She particularly liked this clearing by the lake." He pointed. "For picnics."

"I suppose you don't have any food in your pockets."

For a moment, with the sparkle in her eye and the archness in her voice, she reminded him of their conversations at Netherfield, and he was thrilled to hear the energy in her voice. "Unfortunately not. But perhaps another day."

She smiled briefly, then looked concerned as if suddenly realizing the impropriety of the suggestion, and added quickly, "I think Juliette would enjoy a picnic."

"She would," he agreed. He realized that during their walk, they had not discussed his daughter. He had not been acting as her employer. He had been speaking as if she was still Miss Bennet of Longbourn. He had been sharing too much information with her and asking too much from her.

She looked around. "Perhaps we should turn back."

"Yes, that would be wise," he agreed, but as he looked at the path, he realized how far they had gone. "But we have passed the half way point."

"Oh no," she said. "What time is it?"

He looked at his watch and told her.

She blanched. "We have been walking for more than two hours."

His conscience struck him. "Forgive me," he said. "It is easy to forget the time." Especially when one is having a marvellous time, he thought, but did not say it. "If we walk quickly, we can be back at the house within another hour."

"I suppose there is no other choice."

"No." He wished it didn't matter and that they could continue their walk leisurely, enjoying each other's company, but he knew that would be risking scandal.

But would that be so terrible? No one thought anything amiss when he walked with her at Rosings, but to be gone such a long time, with her employer would be tempting fate.

And as much as he would like to marry her, he would not force her hand.

For the remainder of the walk, they both said little and Elizabeth walked quickly, until she was almost out of breath. He noticed with pleasure that she lengthened her stride to match his.

As they returned to the short path, they were met by one of the footmen. "Sir," the young man said in surprise as he saw Darcy and Elizabeth together.

Darcy knew what he might be thinking and strove to nip any gossip in the bud. "John, would you please escort Miss Bennet back to the house? I am sure they are looking for her at the nursery. She made a wrong turn and took the long path."

Elizabeth looked at him as if surprised by his prevarication, but thankfully she did not correct him.

"Yes, sir," the footman said.

"Good day, Miss Bennet," he said formally, with a bow.

"Yes, sir."

Darcy walked back to the house by another route around the rose gardens and went directly to his office. A few minutes later, Mrs. Reynolds came to the doorway and asked to speak with him. "I heard that Miss Bennet took the long path this morning."

"Yes."

"And that you found her."

He wasn't going to confirm or deny that. "I hope the household ran smoothly without her."

Mrs. Reynold's lips tightened. "She was missed, sir. Juliette was concerned."

"Well, she has returned now, and that is all that matters."

"Perhaps in the future, Miss Bennet should have a

maid accompany her so she doesn't get lost?"

"I don't think that will be necessary."

Mrs. Reynolds would never express it, but he could tell that she was disappointed in him. "I don't want her to go down the wrong path."

He stiffened at the implication that he had been leading her up the garden path. "I don't believe Miss Bennet is any worse for the day's adventure."

"Very good, sir. I wouldn't want her to come to any harm."

"Neither would I."

Mrs. Reynolds considered his words for a moment. "The problem is that a young woman's reputation is so fragile, especially for one in service. I wouldn't want there to be any gossip."

"See that there isn't any," Mr. Darcy said firmly.

"Yes, sir. But you know how some people will talk."

From the look in her eyes, he knew what she was thinking. She wondered if he had lured Elizabeth away to spend time with her. And he had. It wasn't right, but he had enjoyed their walk and had wanted it to continue. He was tempted, and he had briefly succumbed, but he was back to his senses now and would do the right thing. He cleared his throat. "As housekeeper, that is under your supervision," he said coolly. "And I think it is time for me to go to London again."

"Yes, sir."

* * *

Darcy finished his brandy. "Bring me another," he told the steward.

Colonel Fitzwilliam sat across from him. They both sat in dark leather chairs in the panelled room of a private Gentleman's club. "I have never seen you like this. Darcy, what is the matter?"

"For the first time in my life, I don't want to go home to Pemberley." Having Elizabeth in his home was too great a distraction. Every time he saw her, he was reminded that she was not his wife and never would become so. He ran his fingers through his hair.

"What is the problem?" the Colonel asked. "Are there financial difficulties?

Darcy shook his head. "No, I don't want to talk about it."

"I know what you need," the Colonel said. "You need to get out, to do something different. You need to relax."

Darcy downed the other glass – he did not know if it was his second or third – and joined him. "Lead the way, Fitzwilliam," he said. As he stood, his head swam, and he had to take a moment to steady himself.

They took a hansom cab and drove up to a large townhouse. "Is this one of the new gaming establishments?" Darcy asked. "I don't think my head is clear enough to gamble tonight."

"You'll see," the Colonel said pleasantly.

Once inside they were met by a woman with an elaborate headdress topped by ostrich plumes. Her ample bosom seemed on the brink of overflowing her bright green gown. "Ah, Colonel," she said politely. "How good to see you again. I see you've brought a friend?"

In his befuddled state, Darcy realized that they must be at Madame Lucienne's and that this was a house of ill repute. He knew he should be shocked and annoyed with his cousin, but he also thought, Why not? How bad could it be? And perhaps if he could lie with a woman, he would not think about Elizabeth Bennet so often.

He let himself be led upstairs to a room. He sat in a comfortable chair and drank another glass of wine. Within a few minutes a young woman entered. She was a pretty thing with gold hair and too much rouge. As she approached him, he saw that she did not look much older than Georgiana.

He frowned.

"Is there a problem?" the girl asked.

He was disgusted with himself. He could not do this.

He reached for his purse. "Forgive me," he said and handed her a guinea. "I wish to be left alone."

"Is it something I've done?" the girl asked. "Would you prefer someone else?"

The only woman he wished to lie with was back at Pemberley, lying safely in her own virginal bed, but he could not spend time thinking of that. "No, I am fine. Let me know when my friend, the Colonel, is ready to leave. And until then, let me have this room to myself."

"Yes, sir."

CHAPTER TWELVE

While Mr. Darcy was in London, Elizabeth wrote to him daily, offering a brief description of Juliette's day. He was gone three weeks. When he returned, she wondered if he was avoiding her. She saw him even less than she had before, and wondered if he regretted their walk around Pemberley, but she thought it more likely that he was busy with estate affairs. She had learned he owned several properties besides Pemberley and sometimes served as magistrate. She had his permission to read anything in the library, so sometimes after Juliette was asleep, she would go into that large beautiful room and sit. Her father would have loved his book collection.

Life settled into a calm, peaceful pattern.

Until one day when her peace was disrupted by a letter from the Gardiners. Mrs. Sally took care of Juliette so Elizabeth could read her mail in privacy.

She walked out to Pemberley's rose garden and sat on a stone bench to read.

She opened the letter with anticipation, but the first few words astonished her.

Dear Lizzy:

We do not wish to alarm you, but we must tell you that Lydia has eloped with Mr. Wickham. We learned of this from Colonel Forster a week ago. They have been traced as far as London. From her letter, it appears that Lydia thought they were going to Scotland, but Colonel Forster spoke with Mr. Wickham's friend Mr. Denny in Brighton and he does not believe that Wickham planned to marry her. It appears that Mr. Wickham was greatly in debt – primarily gaming debts – and he left Brighton to avoid his creditors.

Mr. Gardiner is still trying to locate them.

Your mother is upset because Lydia may be ruined and because her actions will lessen Kitty and Mary's prospects and reflect poorly on herself as a mother.

As much as I hate to pain you, I thought you should be notified as well.

Please pray for us. I will write more when I have more information.

I hope you are well and enjoying your position at Pemberley.

With all my love,

Elizabeth let the paper fall to her lap. She did not

know what to do. There was nothing she could do. Mr. Gardiner would try to find them, to rescue Lydia, but she knew it would be too late. Stupid, foolish girl. Did she think Wickham would marry her? She had no money to tempt him.

Elizabeth looked up and to her amazement she saw Mr. Darcy approaching her. He must have seen her from one of the house windows.

She pulled out a handkerchief and tried to dry her eyes.

He said, "Miss Bennet, is something amiss?"

She hastily put the letter aside. "I'm sorry. Does Mrs. Sally need me? She was watching Juliette for a few moments."

"It does not matter if she does. You look unwell. What is the matter?"

Elizabeth hesitated, and she tried to stand, but knees trembled under her, so she sat again.

"Can I help you? Is there nothing you could take to give you present relief? A glass of wine perhaps?"

She shook her head and made a feeble attempt at humour. "No, I wouldn't want the other servants to see me drinking during the day."

"Do you need a doctor?"

His kindness was comforting. "No, I am quite well, merely distressed by some dreadful news which I have just received from London."

She burst into tears, then struggled to regain her composure. "Forgive me. It does not matter. There is nothing I can do, so I should not bother you."

"Tell me," he urged. He sat beside her on the bench. It seemed the most natural gesture for him to take her hand in his. "Let me be the judge of what I can or cannot do."

She appreciated the comforting touch. "I have just received a letter from my Aunt Gardiner, with dreadful news. It cannot be concealed from anyone for long. My youngest sister has left all her friends – has eloped – has thrown herself into the power of Mr. Wickham."

Darcy swore.

"Yes, you know him well enough to know the result. She has no money, no connections, nothing that can tempt him to marry her. She is lost forever."

"I am grieved to hear it. Shocked," said Darcy. "But is it absolutely certain?"

"Yes. They left Brighton together about ten days ago and were traced almost to London, but not to Scotland." My uncle is trying to discover them."

"Has he had any success?"

"No, and I doubt he will. Poor stupid Lydia. And now what will happen to Mary and Kitty? It is bad enough to have a sister working as a governess, but they can distance themselves from me because I am only a half relation. Lydia is their full sister. You know how society will react, what people will say."

"Yes, I know."

"Indeed, I am glad to be at Pemberley away from the gossiping tongues."

He asked, "Do you wish to take a leave of absence, to join your family?"

She shook her head. "No, there is nothing I could do to help. I fear I would only be an added burden to my stepmother. She is not taking the news well."

Mr. Darcy was silent for a moment, then said, "Miss Bennet, let me express my sorrow for your distress. I hope that the situation will not turn out to be as bad as you fear."

Elizabeth forced herself to smile. "Thank you, sir. I am sorry I bothered you with my private concerns."

"No. Anything that concerns anyone at Pemberley, concerns me." He patted her hand briefly, then withdrew and stood. "I will leave you to your privacy."

"Thank you."

His words were awkward, stiff, and Elizabeth thought that this was another reason she was glad she had not agreed to marry him. How would he have felt to be related to such a girl as Lydia? She watched as he returned to the house.

After taking a few minutes to compose herself, she forced herself to dry her eyes and return to her work. She played spilikins with Juliette in one of the gardens. That evening after Juliette was asleep, Georgiana asked her to join her in playing cards. Elizabeth was grateful for the distraction. As she spoke with Miss Darcy, she could not help but think of Wickham. What a blackguard he was – first trying to elope with Georgiana, and now running off with Lydia.

Georgiana informed her that Mr. Darcy had gone to London.

"Again? But he just recently returned."

"Yes, I don't know what it is," Miss Darcy said. "Some business in Town, I assume. He does not tell me. I don't know when he will return."

Mr. Darcy was gone for another two weeks. As he had requested, she continued to write him daily of Juliette's lessons and sent the letters to his London townhouse. She wished she could thank him for his kindness when he came to her in the garden, but she felt that it would be inappropriate to remind him. In the end, she wrote calmly of the weather, Juliette's health and their daily activities.

More than once she wished she could ask about his health as well, but did not.

Elizabeth heard nothing more from her Aunt Gardiner and worried about Lydia. But there was nothing she could do to make the situation better, so she tried to focus on her work. She enjoyed playing with Juliette and spent some additional time with Miss Darcy. Sometimes in the evenings they read together, played the pianoforte or worked on needlework.

"Miss Bennet," Miss Darcy said one evening. "It is such a joy to have you in the house. Thank you for spending your evenings with me. I did not realize before how lonely I was, craving female companionship. How marvellous it must have been for you to have four sisters."

"Most of the time, it was a blessing," Elizabeth said. "But sometimes it was a sore trial. It is impossible for five young women to share a house without some upsets and misunderstandings. But I was very close to my sister Jane."

"The one who died."

"Yes. She was the best of sisters."

A few nights later, Elizabeth was putting Juliette to bed when Mr. Darcy returned. He had not changed from his journey and still wore a long travelling coat.

"Sir," she said when she saw him standing in the doorway to his daughter's bedroom. "You startled me."

"Forgive me. I merely wished to see Juliette."

"She is well. She just recently fell asleep."

Mr. Darcy lowered his voice. "Then I would not wish to wake her." He glanced at his daughter. He reached down and gently smoothed her hair. "She looks like an angel."

"She is an angel. Most of the time."

He smiled at her. "Come now, Miss Bennet," he said. "She has a temper, too, and that does not bother me. I would rather she have some spirit than none at all. Has she given you any grief while I was gone?"

"No, not at all."

"I'm glad to hear it."

Elizabeth stood back, stepping into the hallway to give him more privacy. "I will leave you alone."

"No," he said quickly. "There is no need, and in truth, I would like to speak with you briefly, if I may. Privately."

She supposed he wished to discuss Juliette's education or care. She waited.

He stepped out into the hallway to join her. He quietly closed Juliette's door.

They stood only a few inches apart. Elizabeth held

a candle and in the flickering light she scanned his face. He looked tired, as if the trip to London had exhausted him. Her heart was touched, and she wished he would take better care for himself.

He asked, "Have you heard from your aunt and uncle? About Lydia?"

She was surprised by the question but was pleased that he cared enough to ask. "No, sir."

"Then I have preceded them," he said. "Normally, I would wait for them to inform you, but I think you would prefer to hear her news as soon as possible, even if it does come from me."

"You have news? But how?"

"Yes, your sister Lydia is now married to Mr. Wickham."

Elizabeth knew she should be happy for her sister because marriage was better than the alternative, but she did not think Lydia would fare well. "Married? Are you certain? Is it not just a rumour?"

"No. She married two days ago."

She frowned. "And how did you learn of it?"

"I was there at the church."

Elizabeth was stunned. "You? But why?"

"Your uncle and I arranged the matter. I thought you would like to know as soon as possible, to relieve your mind."

"Thank you." Her mind was now in a whirl. Mr. Darcy and her uncle arranging the matter together? "I thank you sir, for your assistance."

"I did very little. I merely helped your uncle find the man. I knew Wickham's haunts of old and was able to track him down."

"Like a fox."

Mr. Darcy smiled. "I regret that I was unable to set my hounds on him."

It was all too much to take in. Lydia married, and Darcy had arranged it. "Do you think she will be happy with him? No, forgive me, that is a foolish question. Naturally she won't be happy."

"No, he will not make a good husband," Darcy said seriously. "But she was determined. We offered her the option of leaving him. We could have concocted a story of her visiting relatives, but she would not take it."

"But how did you convince him to marry her?" The moment the words were out of her mouth, she answered her own question. "I assume he had to be paid. My poor uncle," she said and then looked at him with sudden comprehension. "You paid him."

Mr. Darcy looked uncomfortable, but he did not deny it. "I have a larger income than your uncle."

"How much did it take?"

"You don't want to know."

She lifted her chin slightly. "You don't want to tell me."

"You are correct. I don't. I regret that I told you anything at all. I should have let the news come from your uncle." His words were firm, but there was a softness about his eyes.

"I don't know how I can ever repay you."

He shook his head. "There is no need." He smiled wryly. "But if you insist, I could take it out of your salary."

"At a hundred pounds a year, I suspect I would be your indentured servant until I die."

He nodded. "It is all part of my plan to keep the best governess Juliette has ever had."

"It is not difficult to be the best governess when I'm the only one she's ever had."

"True."

Elizabeth knew he was trying to be kind, but the reality of it still concerned her. "Mr. Darcy, you make light of it, but I know it must have distressed you. I am sorry that you were involved in this sordid matter."

"I chose to involve myself."

"I know, and I cannot help but wonder at it."

"Why? Don't you know that I would do almost

anything for you, for your happiness?"

Elizabeth flushed, alarmed by the warmth of his words.

But even as he spoke, he seemed to regret it and pulled back emotionally. When he continued, his emotions were banked and guarded. "Forgive me, Miss Bennet. I hope I would do the same for any of my employees. I want Pemberley to be a happy home."

"I understand. Thank you again, Mr. Darcy," she said formally.

"You are most welcome, Miss Bennet. Good night." He turned to leave.

Elizabeth walked to her bedroom and closed the door quietly. She had so much to think about. When Mr. Darcy had appeared in the doorway, for a moment her heart had warmed and she knew she had missed him.

She thought of her aunt's advice. She must be careful. Over time, she had grown to love his daughter, his sister, and his house.

She did not want to fall in love with him as well.

If only he would be the disagreeable, arrogant man she'd first thought he was. It was going to be difficult to keep from falling in love with the intelligent, kind, and reliable man she had discovered him to be.

Elizabeth sighed. She wished that she could tell Jane and share her misery. For misery it was. For even if she was falling in love with him, it did not change the reality of her situation. She was his daughter's governess. And he would never want to marry her now that she was related to Wickham.

Elizabeth sighed. She wished that doing the right thing was not so difficult.

* * *

Darcy cursed himself for being a fool. He should not have sought Elizabeth out. Why had he told her of Lydia's marriage? Because at some level he had wanted her appreciation.

When she asked how she could repay him, it had taken all of his self-control not to answer her honestly:

Marry me. Give yourself to me. Become mine for today and always.

But he could not do that. He refused to play upon her sympathies or to buy her regard.

And yet, in that instant he was tempted.

He must strengthen his resolve. He must not speak to her alone again, especially not at night in a hallway with the flickering light of the candle illuminating her beautiful face and the curve of her throat.

He must keep his distance.

He went to his office and sat down at his desk. The pile of correspondence and bills was damning. As much as he had been glad to help Elizabeth's younger sister, he had spent too much time away from Pemberley lately. Although he had an excellent steward, the estate would not run itself. There were decisions that only he could make.

He tugged on a bell pull and a servant appeared in the doorway. "Sir?" the young man asked.

Darcy looked up. "Have Cook prepare me a cold supper on a tray."

"Yes, sir."

Darcy sighed and opened the first envelope. Work would be the answer to his troubles. Pemberley would be his salvation.

* * *

With Mr. Darcy's return, Miss Darcy spent her evenings with him and not with Elizabeth. Elizabeth spent more time reading and decided to improve her French. When she saw Mr. Darcy, their conversations were brief and primarily on Juliette and her education.

Eventually summer turned to autumn. Mrs.

Gardiner wrote that Kitty had a beau, one of Mr. Gardiner's distant cousins. They planned to marry in the spring, once his business was more established. As for Lydia, Wickham had joined a regiment in the North.

Elizabeth was pleased to hear the news, but sometimes it felt as if her prior life was a distant dream. Instead of balls and shopping, she thought more of Juliette and the quiet pleasures of Pemberley. In her free hours, she often spoke to the head gardener or Mrs. Reynolds, learning the history of the house.

And gradually as the weeks passed, as she thought of Jane or her father, she could remember them with joy and not as much pain.

* * *

Darcy returned home from a brief trip visiting some of his other properties and was met by Mrs. Reynolds. "Oh sir, what an uproar. Miss Juliette has been ill with the croup. Dr. Jamison was here. He bled her and gave her a draught, but she is still doing poorly."

"How long has she been ill?"

"Several days."

He had been travelling, not staying anywhere

more than a day, so that there had been no way for Elizabeth's letters to reach him. He handed his coat and gloves to a servant and hurried up to the nursery.

Darcy did not believe in doctors. He had seen what they had done to Anne over the years, and he did not think any of their ministrations had helped her. He often thought she would have been much happier to have moved to the south of Italy with warmer weather and better food. But she, raised by her mother, believed everything the doctors told her- even when they contradicted themselves. She was a dutiful patient and ultimately she had died. He entered the nursery and saw Elizabeth and Mrs. Sally beside his daughter's bed.

Juliette looked pale and listless. When she coughed, it was a horrible rattling sound as if the cough would tear her body in two. "Papa," she said weakly.

He sat on the edge of the bed and kissed her forehead. "Hello, dearest. I am sorry you are feeling poorly."

Juliette did not have the energy to converse with him but seemed pleased to see him.

After a few minutes, he spoke privately with Elizabeth in the hall. "What brought this on?"

"I don't know. She has had a cold for the past two

weeks, but yesterday it took a turn for the worse. Her cough is better in the day, but worse at night."

At that moment, Juliette started coughing again, a long drawn out spell that lasted several minutes and made him fear she would not be able to breathe. She cried and gasped and made a frightening barking sound as she coughed. When the coughing fit finally subsided, Mrs. Sally wiped her face with a damp cloth. "There, there," she comforted.

Darcy asked, "What is to be done?"

"I don't know," Elizabeth said. "Dr. Jamison does not seem concerned, he says that all children go through this, but I hate to have him bleed her again. Her little arm is so thin. I remember when all the Lucases had the same whooping cough, all at once."

"Did they live?'

"Yes."

"Then tell me what they did."

"Steam. They put all the children in one room and filled it with pots of boiling water. It seemed to relieve the cough."

"Then that's what we will do as well."

"They also used a mixture of rum and turpentine to rub on the children's chests and limbs."

"I will talk to Mrs. Reynolds and have it made immediately."

It was the work of an hour to move Juliette to a smaller bedroom and set up pots of boiling water around the bed. Servants were kept busy bringing pots of hot water from the kitchen. A large blaze was built in the fireplace to keep the water boiling.

Elizabeth and Mrs. Sally took turns sitting by the young girl, caring for her. Darcy arranged for another servant to assist them. He stood back, watching his daughter fight for breath and thought of Anne. Anne's ailments had been different, but he couldn't bear to have Juliette die as well.

Elizabeth, seeing his concern, approached him. "Mr. Darcy," she said kindly. "Perhaps it would be best if you left the sick room."

"I wish there was something I could do."

"You have already done it. Let us care for her. We will let you know if her condition worsens."

He nodded. "Thank you."

The next few days were difficult, but the treatment Elizabeth suggested seemed to turn the tide. By the third night, Juliette was able to sleep without being woken by coughing fits every few hours. Darcy who had been kept apprised of her progress and had visited her several times a day, came by near midnight to check on her before retiring to bed. The fire in the fireplace had died down, but the room was still hot and damp. There was one servant asleep on a cot in the corner of the room. Elizabeth Bennet sat in a high backed chair beside the bed. She was asleep as well, her head tilted to one side. Her hair was a damp riot of curls pulled back into an untidy bun. One of the buttons on her black high necked gown was undone, exposing a tiny v of skin at her throat.

She looked so different from the carefree young woman who had danced with him at Netherfield, but he still found her beautiful.

He sighed, not wanting to wake her, and feared she would have a crick in her neck by morning. He knew she'd slept as little as he the past few days.

Darcy sat in another chair for a few minutes, watching the steady even breathing of his daughter and periodically glancing at Elizabeth as well.

He loved her. Her kindness to his daughter and her strength in the midst of trial had solidified his feelings completely. He knew now beyond all doubt that she was the only woman in the world for him. He would never find her equal. If she would not marry him, he could not bring himself to marry another, even if that meant he would not provide an heir for Pemberley.

He was astonished with himself. He had spent his life doing what was best for Pemberley.

But for once, he would not do his duty. For once, he would do what he wished.

Unless he could somehow convince Elizabeth to marry him, he would not provide an heir for Pemberley.

Which meant that his cousin Julian Darcy would inherit.

Darcy ran his fingers through his hair. He did not know Julian well, but what he did know was not promising. Julian was a charming man, worldly, caught up in the vulgarities of society. But then, Darcy thought, he had not the opportunity to be taught differently. Perhaps if he was invited to Pemberley, he could learn management for the estate and be better prepared to be its owner. Without training, he would be more likely to ruin Pemberley, and Darcy refused to let that happen.

Now that he had a plan, he felt better. Once Juliette was well again, he would invite the man to Pemberley. Dr. Jamison had said that these sort of coughing fits could linger for weeks, gradually reducing. Perhaps she would be well by Christmas.

Eventually he stood to return to his bedchambers. He smoothed Juliette's sheets and kissed her forehead. On impulse he reached over and kissed Elizabeth's forehead as well.

She stirred which made him catch his breath in fear that she would wake, but she did not. "Good night, Elizabeth," he said quietly. "God bless you." He blew out the candles and closed the door behind him.

CHAPTER THIRTEEN

Juliette's health improved throughout the autumn. She spent most of her time indoors, taking only brief walks outside. Her riding lessons were postponed until the spring. With the additional academic lessons, she learned to read and began writing sums. Mrs. Sally declared that she was the most intelligent child she had ever known. Elizabeth had to hide a laugh when Mr. Darcy pretended to be slighted. "What of me, Mrs. Sally?" he had joked.

One day Elizabeth came into the library and found Darcy sitting in a chair with Juliette on his lap. They were reading a story together. He was patient and helped her with the difficult words. Elizabeth's heart seemed to leap to her throat and she remembered her father doing the same for her. "Excuse me," she said quietly, not wanting to disturb them.

She was so proud of them both – Juliette for

learning to read and Mr Darcy for taking the time to help her. It was moments like these that made her work as a governess meaningful.

Mr. Darcy had originally planned to visit Rosings Park again in October, but did not feel that Juliette was well enough to travel, so there was talk of Lady Catherine joining them for Christmas. Elizabeth did not look forward to that event.

On a happier note, she heard that her Aunt Gardiner had given birth to a healthy daughter.

In November, Darcy invited his cousin Julian Darcy and Mr. Bingley to visit. Elizabeth asked Georgiana if she was acquainted with her cousin Julian.

"Not well, but I hear he is very handsome."

* * *

Julian looked out the library window. "Damme, Darcy, who is that young woman on the lawn?"

"That is Miss Bennet, Juliette's governess."

"She is a handsome woman. When can I meet her?"

Darcy should have known this would happen. "You will not meet her. Stay away from her, Julian. Your job is to learn more about Pemberley, not to trifle with the servants."

Julian continued to observe her. "She dresses all in black. Is she a Methodist?"

"No, she is in mourning."

"Even better. Perhaps I can give her some consolation."

"Do not harass her."

Julian laughed. "I am beginning to recognize your Master of Pemberley tone of voice. Why are you so concerned, Darcy? Have you reserved her for yourself?"

Darcy stiffened. "I do not find that comment even remotely amusing."

"Can't you take a joke?"

"Not when it concerns the welfare of my employees. Being owner of Pemberley is not just a matter of property and rents. I am responsible for dozens of people on the estate, not to mention my tenants. Nearly every decision I make affects the quality of their lives. So no, I don't joke about taking advantage of one of my employees."

Julian said, "Forgive me. I can see I have a lot to learn."

Darcy did not want to lecture him, but could not seem to help himself. He hoped now that he would live a long time so that his cousin would not inherit before he was an older and much wiser man.

As Georgiana had predicted, Julian Darcy was a handsome man, tall like Mr. Darcy, but with lighter hair. While he was visiting, Elizabeth was not invited to the family dinners, but she had met him briefly once when they were both in the library. He had asked her about the book she was reading and recommended another.

She did not think much of it until a few days later, when she returned to the library to exchange volumes. She had not noticed that he was in the room, but then he approached her. "Ah, Miss Bennet," he said smoothly. "We meet again. If I didn't know better, I might think you had planned to meet me here."

There was something in his tone that reminded her of Wickham. She shivered and quickly put away the volume of poetry in her hand. "I'm sorry to disturb you. If you'll excuse me –"

But he caught her arm rather than let her walk past him. "You do disturb me," he said with a smile. "You are a very beautiful woman, did you know that?"

She tried to pull her arm from his grasp but he held firm. "Please unhand me, Mr. Darcy," she said, striving to remain calm.

"You don't mean that," he said. "You can't mean that." He reached up to touch the hair on the side of her face. She tried to turn her face away, but he leaned forward to kiss her.

For a moment his lips were against hers. Elizabeth twisted and pushed against him with her left hand but it was futile. He was taller and stronger than she. She reached behind herself to find a book - the first book she could find - and brought it up against the side of his head in a sharp blow, boxing his right ear.

Surprised, he drew back and swore at her. "Damme, if you aren't a vixen."

He momentarily loosened his hold and she jerked her arm free. She ran to the library door and out into the hallway. She turned a corner and nearly collided with Mr. Darcy, her Mr. Darcy.

"Elizabeth," he gasped when he saw her, then quickly corrected himself. "Miss Bennet, is there a problem?"

"Yes, I mean – I don't know," Elizabeth said quickly, her thoughts racing. "Your cousin." She flushed, not knowing what to say.

Darcy's countenance darkened as he noticed her dishevelled state. "What did he do?"

"He found me in the library. He kissed me."

"I will kill him."

"No," she said quickly and touched his arm. "Perhaps he thought he was flirting with me, but I did not wa–"

"Did you encourage him?"

She flushed at the implication. Did he think so poorly of her? "No, sir."

"Then he should not have accosted you."

Elizabeth did not want to cause trouble between the two men, but she could not help it. "I will go back to the nursery now and tidy myself."

"And my cousin will be leaving today," Darcy said firmly.

She looked at him for a moment, grateful yet again for his kindnesses to her. "Thank you." She hurried up the north staircase. She thought of Miss Barnes and her tales. She knew now how quickly situations could change. If Mr. Julian Darcy had come to her room, she would have had to use her knife.

At dinner, she heard from the servants that Mr. Julian had left earlier that afternoon. "I thought he was going to stay until the new year," one of the footmen said.

"He had obligations in Town," Mrs. Reynolds said firmly, silencing the conversation.

* * *

After Julian left, Darcy thought often of the situation. Julian said, "It was only a kiss, Darcy. You take it much too seriously."

"And you don't take it seriously enough."

To some extent, he was envious of Julian for he had taken what Darcy himself wanted. Darcy wished he could take Elizabeth in his arms and kiss her. But he had promised her that if she would join his household that he would not take advantage of the situation to further his pursuit. And even if he could propose a third time, he was afraid that she would say no again, and then go away, leaving him with nothing. Wasn't it better to keep her in his house for now than to risk losing her forever?

Bingley arrived a few days after Julian left. Darcy was glad to see him, but was astonished to learn that Bingley had brought his sister Caroline as well. "Welcome to Pemberley," he said smoothly.

"Oh Mr. Darcy," Miss Bingley said. "It is so wonderful to be at Pemberley again."

Darcy was amazed to think that he had ever considered Miss Bingley to be a potential wife. She was so proud and insincere. He asked Mrs. Reynolds to show her to a room so she could refresh herself after her long journey.

"I'm sorry," Bingley said after she had left the room. "But she didn't want to stay in Town by herself. My sister Louisa and her husband are visiting his family. I thought you wouldn't mind."

Darcy realized if Bingley thought that, he didn't know him at all. In the past year, they had not seen as much of each other, and their friendship was lessening. Darcy smiled and said, "Don't worry. Georgiana will enjoy the company."

"Thank you," Bingley said.

* * *

Miss Bingley insisted on visiting the nursery to see Juliette, and upon entering the room, she was stunned to see Elizabeth. "Miss Bennet," she exclaimed. "What are you doing at Pemberley?"

Elizabeth set aside the book she was reading and stood. "I am Miss Juliette's governess."

"Oh, that explains your atrocious gown," Miss Bingley said with a superior tone. "And yes, I do remember hearing that your father had died. My condolences for your loss."

Elizabeth thanked her, not because she thought Miss Bingley's professions were sincere, but because she wanted to teach Juliette proper manners.

Miss Bingley handed Juliette a wrapped box. "I

have a present for you."

Juliette, suddenly shy, stood behind Elizabeth's skirt.

"This is Miss Bingley, Juliette," Elizabeth prompted her young charge. "I don't know if you remember her, but her brother is one of your father's good friends."

"Of course you remember me," Miss Bingley insisted, which made Juliette shrink back.

"Can you thank her for the present?" Elizabeth prompted.

"Thank you," Juliette said with a curtsey and dutifully accepted the package.

"Aren't you going to open it?" Miss Bingley demanded.

Juliette stood, indecisive, looking fearfully at Elizabeth.

"I will help you," Mrs. Sally said and walked with Juliette to a small table.

"I don't know what you've done to her," Miss Bingley said in a tone that carried throughout the room. "She used to be a most friendly little girl."

"She has not been well lately," Elizabeth said quietly. "Perhaps she is tired."

"Oh, so she takes after her mother, does she?" Miss Bingley said. "That's a shame."

Elizabeth tried to change the subject. "Miss Bingley, it has been nearly a year since we last saw each other. Have you ever gone back to Netherfield?"

"No. Charles has no interest in it and is thinking of giving up the place altogether. I am hoping that he finds a new property here in Derbyshire."

So that she would be closer to Mr. Darcy, Elizabeth thought. "It is lovely here."

"How long have you been working for Mr. Darcy?" Miss Bingley asked but did not listen to her answer because Juliette had opened the gift, and she wanted to see her reaction.

It was a little miniature set of china dishes.

"How clever," Elizabeth said, admiring one of the tiny delicate tea cups.

"For your dolls," Miss Bingley said to Juliette.

Juliette said, "Yes, thank you."

Later that evening, Miss Bingley expressed her thoughts to Darcy, "I was astonished to see Miss Bennet in the nursery, Darcy."

"Miss Bennet?" Bingley said with interest.

"Yes, she is Juliette's governess now."

"I would like to speak with her," Bingley said, "If I may."

Caroline looked annoyed. "Why would you want to do that? We are no longer her neighbours."

"No, but I would like to express my condolences for the loss of her sister."

Darcy said, "I will arrange for her to join us for breakfast, if you wish."

"I would appreciate that, thank you. It's difficult to believe that it has only been a year since we were all dancing at Netherfield. It seems like a lifetime ago."

Darcy watched his friend with sympathy, wondering if he had truly loved Jane Bennet. He might not be married to Elizabeth, but at least she was alive and in his house. Poor Bingley would never have the chance of seeing Jane Bennet again.

"How greatly Miss Bennet has changed," Miss Bingley said. "At first, I did not recognize her. She has grown so thin and sickly."

"She is a little slimmer," Darcy agreed.

"It is a shame. I know when we were in Hertfordshire, she was considered one of the local beauties. But now, no one would look twice at her."

Mr. Darcy could not keep silent. "I disagree. Wherever Miss Bennet is, she will be admired."

"But why? I must confess that I see no beauty in her. Her face is too thin; her complexion has no brilliancy and her features are not at all handsome. Her teeth are tolerable, but nothing extraordinary. And her eyes, which have sometimes been called fine, seem to have a sharp, shrewish look."

Darcy turned away, determined to avoid the conversation.

But Miss Bingley persisted. "I see you agree with me. I remember your saying one night when we were at Netherfield, 'She a beauty – I should as soon call her mother a wit.'"

His temper flared. "Miss Bingley," he said coolly. "I do not think it appropriate for you to disparage a young woman in my employ. But for the record, whatever I thought of her appearance when we first met, that has changed. I now consider her one of the handsomest women of my acquaintance. And more importantly, she is the one woman I have chosen to care for my daughter. I hold her in the highest esteem."

Miss Bingley looked pained. "No doubt she is an excellent governess."

"She is," Darcy agreed. "And I would rather not discuss her further."

* * *

Elizabeth was pleased to see Mr. Bingley at breakfast. He was as she remembered, pleasant and amiable. He expressed his condolences for Jane's and her father's death and she sensed that he was sincere.

She could no longer hate him for abandoning Jane. He was a good man, perhaps too easily persuaded by his friend, but that was his nature. He said that he often remembered the months he'd spent at Netherfield and considered them the happiest days of his life.

She said, "I hope you will find more happy days in the future."

He asked about her work. "Do you enjoy being a governess?"

She gave an arch look at Mr. Darcy, who was observing their conversation closely. "Come now, Mr. Bingley, that is unfair. How can I be completely honest with my employer listening?"

Darcy smiled. "I can leave the room, if you wish to malign me."

"Oh no, sir. If I malign you, it will be to your face."

Miss Georgiana's eyes widened at this repartee and Elizabeth knew she was not acting appropriately. "Forgive me," she said quickly. "I was merely joking. You are an excellent employer. Mr. Bingley, I am very happy here."

"Do you miss your family?"

Elizabeth made herself smile. "In a way, I feel that Pemberley and the people here have become a second family."

Miss Bingley interjected. "That is good. I think a household runs most efficiently when the servants are happy." She emphasized the word 'servants.' "And the best masters are like parents, don't you agree, Mr. Darcy?"

"I would never so presume, Miss Bingley," he said. "I may be Master of Pemberley, but I do not to control their private lives."

"But you take an interest."

"I take an interest in many things, but I hope I still respect everyone's autonomy and privacy."

"Indeed," Mr. Bingley interjected. "Sometimes that is difficult when you wish to be helpful, but don't want to be offensive."

Elizabeth smiled. She doubted that Mr. Bingley had ever offended anyone in his life, but it was not her place to comment. She excused herself so she could return to the nursery.

"I hope I will see you again, before I leave," Mr. Bingley said.

Miss Bingley glared at him.

Elizabeth looked briefly at her employer. "That is up to Mr. Darcy."

He frowned. "You may speak to Mr. Bingley, if you wish."

"Thank you." She did not plan to make a habit of it, but it would be good to see him one more time. Seeing him and talking of Netherfield had been good for her spirits, reminding her of happier times.

* * *

Darcy began counting the days until Bingley would leave. As much as he liked his friend, he disliked his sister and he could not bear to watch Elizabeth speak with him. When she saw Bingley, her face had lightened and she had almost laughed with him. It was like a slap in the face, reminding him that she admired and cared for Bingley in a way that she had never cared for him. She was comfortable with Bingley, and her natural wit had returned. For a moment, she had begun to tease him as well, until she thought better of it.

Darcy swore. He did not want to be jealous of his friend, but he was. He wanted him gone, away from Elizabeth. For all his talk about respecting her autonomy, he wanted her all to himself. He wanted to be everything to her: master, husband, lover.

But this was madness.

He went riding, and when that was insufficient to restore his equanimity, he ran around the long path. It had been so many years since he had last attempted it that he had to walk parts of it, but he returned to Pemberley, sweaty and tired.

At dinner his sister asked him if he was feeling well. "I am fine," he lied.

CHAPTER FOURTEEN

Lady Catherine de Bourgh descended upon Pemberley with an entourage more suitable to Princess Charlotte: three carriages and a small army of servants. From the conversations below stairs, Elizabeth could tell that the household staff disliked her, but they were too loyal to Mr. Darcy to admit it.

Rather than come to the nursery, Lady Catherine demanded that Juliette be brought to her suite of rooms. She specifically stated that she wished to see her granddaughter without Miss Bennet. "I will speak to her governess, later." Elizabeth did not know what that meant, but arranged for Mrs. Sally to accompany Juliette.

The next few days were busy with Christmas preparations. Juliette was happily distracted and did not want to spend time with her lessons, so Elizabeth let her run and play. Blessedly, Juliette had regained her health and was no longer coughing.

Elizabeth sat by herself, reflecting that this was her first Christmas away from home, but since her father's death, she did not have a home. Longbourn seemed a distant memory. And although she would enjoy visiting her Aunt and Uncle Gardiner, their home was not home, either.

I suppose Pemberley is my home now, she thought.

A few days after she arrived, Lady Catherine requested a private interview with Miss Bennet. Elizabeth walked down the servant's staircase to the second floor where Lady Catherine was staying.

"Ah, Miss Bennet," Lady Catherine said when she entered the room. "Please sit down."

Elizabeth obeyed.

"I do not approve of my son-in-law hiring you as Juliette's governess," she began bluntly. "But she is growing well and you appear to be competent."

"Your praise is hardly won, so I thank you."

"I am not finished. I am sorry for you that your father's death reduced your circumstances, but I do not think it wise for you to be in this house as a servant when a year before, you could have come as a guest. It is highly irregular and fraught with complications."

Elizabeth said, "It is a change, yes, but it was Mr. Darcy's choice."

"Do not interrupt me. I will let you know when you can speak."

Elizabeth realized that as rude as Lady Catherine had been to her before, she intended to be even ruder now that she was in service and deemed socially inferior. She steeled herself for the worst.

"I believe Darcy offered you the position out of kindness, but it was foolhardy and short sighted. And although you may be an excellent governess, that does not mean I approve of you getting beyond your station."

"I thought that by becoming a governess I had lowered my station."

"That is not what I meant. I refer to the rumours that you intend to marry my son-in-law."

Elizabeth gasped. "I know of no such rumours."

Lady Catherine snorted. "I find that difficult to believe."

"And rumours are merely that – unsubstantiated gossip."

"I have heard it from his cousin Julian."

"His cousin Julian is mistaken."

"Can you deny that you have set your cap at him? That you conspire to marry him and become Mistress of Pemberley?"

Elizabeth stiffened. "Are you against Mr. Darcy marrying again, or are you against him marrying me?"

"He is a man. I assume that eventually he will want to marry again, but he deserves a woman in his same station. Preferably a woman with wealth and position."

"I am a gentleman's daughter."

"The daughter of an innkeeper. And you have numerous connections in trade. I have heard of your stepmother making a fool of herself in London."

Elizabeth knew this was most likely true. "Lady Catherine," she said calmly. "You are concerned for no reason. Your son-in-law is my employer, and he appears satisfied with my work, that is all."

"Are you engaged to him?"

"No, I am not."

"And will you promise not to marry him if he does ask?'

Since he had already asked twice and she had foolishly declined his offer twice, she could not believe he would ask again. "I do not know how to answer that question. I am sorry, Lacy Catherine. I know you do not approve of me, but don't you want your son-in-law and granddaughter to be happy?"

"And you think you will make them happy?"

She would not answer that. "Does it matter whom your son chooses as long as the woman is a good mother to your granddaughter? What does rank or wealth matter if the woman is unkind?"

Lady Catherine sputtered.

"I am sorry your daughter Anne was sickly and died before her due time. I hope she was happy in her marriage to Mr. Darcy."

"They were meant for each other."

"And did she love her daughter?"

"What sort of question is this? Naturally she loved her."

"Then she would want a kind mother for her. Lady Catherine, you, if anyone, should know that money and position cannot buy happiness. Money cannot bring your daughter back. I hope that someday you can be at peace with her death."

"No one understands the pain that I feel."

"I agree. I don't believe anyone can completely understand another's pain, but I recently lost my sister and my father, and for months I felt as if I was dead inside. Nothing mattered, nothing had meaning. But gradually, I have learned to enjoy life again, and much of that came from caring for your granddaughter. Juliette is such a bright, sweet girl."

Lady Catherine's countenance changed. "I want to

spend more time with her, but Darcy doesn't like to visit."

"Can you blame him? By being so negative, you push him away. He will do his duty, but he will not love you."

"You express your opinion very decidedly. How can you know this?"

"I care for your granddaughter, Lady Catherine. I want her to have a happy family."

"I do not want you to be her mother."

"I understand that, and I sympathize. But do not make yourself unhappy with unreasonable expectations. Your son-in-law is a good man. If he chooses to marry again, you will have no say in the matter. I believe you would do better to accept that fact and be happy for him."

"So you are determined to have him."

Elizabeth was frustrated. She had tried to reason with Lady Catherine, but that woman was beyond reasoning. "I have said no such thing. I will continue to act as I see fit to bring about my own happiness. But rest assured, I will also take your granddaughter and son-in-law's happiness into consideration as well."

"Then you do care for them."

"Yes." Heaven help her, she did. And if Mr. Darcy

was foolish enough to propose to her a third time, she would not say no. If he did not mind her vulgar family, she would not let it bother her.

"Then I will have to hope that you are wise enough to remain their governess and not aspire to something greater. You may go now. I have nothing further to say to you."

Elizabeth went up to the nursery to speak briefly to Mrs. Sally. "How was her ladyship?" the other woman asked. "Did she want to talk privately about Miss Juliette?"

"Yes," Elizabeth said, not giving any further details. "But I would still like to take a walk this morning, if I may. Would you please stay with Miss Juliette?"

"Take as long as you'd like," Mrs. Sally said. "I'm teaching Miss Juliette how to sew."

"Excellent," Elizabeth said to them both, and quickly left the house. She felt that she needed to be alone, outside, to clear her mind.

She wore a long pelisse and cloak and knitted mittens on her hands, but it was still very cold. But the air was crisp and bright. It had snowed a week before, but the paths were mostly clear.

She walked to the rose garden which was primarily brown twigs and thorns.

"Miss Bennet!"

She turned and saw that Mr. Bingley had come outside to join her. He wore a long coat that he had not finished buttoning. "May I join you?" he asked. His breath was white.

"You may," she said. "But I fear it may be too cold to stay out long."

"What I have to say will not take long." He offered his arm, she took it, and together they walked around the rose garden. Her boots made a crunching sound on the cold pebbles and icy brown leaves.

She waited for him to speak, and when he did, he seemed flustered. "I don't know how to say this, actually."

She smiled. "Mr. Bingley, we are friends. You do not need to stand on ceremony with me. Whatever you wish to say, I will gladly hear and not judge you if it comes out awkwardly."

He nodded. "I know that. That's why I'm here."

Again she waited.

"I loved your sister Jane," he said finally. "The greatest regret of my life is that I stayed in London and didn't come back to that dinner with your family."

Elizabeth's eyes grew misty. "Thank you for telling me. And she loved you, too."

"Did she hate me for staying away?"

"No, she always spoke of you kindly."

"That was her nature."

Elizabeth nodded. "Yes."

They walked for a minute in silence. Elizabeth said, "Life is so precarious. None of us know how long we will live. I think the secret to happiness is to appreciate what we have. And Jane did appreciate you."

He nodded, and his voice was harsh with emotion. "Thank you."

They walked for a few more minutes. Mr. Bingley said, "I never thought to see you become a governess."

"No. Neither did I."

"But you are happy?"

Yes, in her way, she was. "Yes."

"Seeing you again has brought make so many memories, so many feelings."

"I feel the same."

There was another lull in the conversation. Then he said, "Miss Bennet. Forgive me, but I have wondered if you would consider marrying me."

Elizabeth blinked, completely stunned. Her stepmother would be thrilled. "Mr. Bingley," she said. "Thank you for that generous thought, but I must decline. You still care for my sister."

"I think I will always care for her."

"And that is right. But later, you will fall in love again."

"I think I am falling in love with you."

She looked at this dear, gentle man, and her heart was touched. "I am nothing like my sister. I do not have her sweet temper."

"But you are charming."

"No, Mr. Bingley. I would make you a miserable wife. You would want me to be more like Jane and I would –" She caught herself. She could not say *I would want you to be more like Mr. Darcy.* "But I thank you sincerely for the compliment."

"So there is no hope for me?"

"There is always hope, Mr. Bingley. But I think you must find something of value to do with your life. Perhaps you should run an estate like Mr. Darcy, or go into politics, or return to Trade. I believe that a person must be busy or melancholy can destroy them. A life without purpose is hardly worth living."

He nodded. "There has to be more to life than spending money."

"Exactly."

"And you have found your purpose in teaching Miss Juliette."

"Yes."

He took her hand and bought it up to his lips to kiss it and was startled by the fuzzy knit of her mittens. He smiled at the absurdity. "This is hardly romantic."

"It is too cold outside to be romantic," she said firmly. "Let us be friends, instead."

He reached over and touched her nose. "Your nose is red," he said.

She laughed. "And yours is white. Let us go inside before we both catch our death of colds."

He said, "I wouldn't mind dying if I thought I would see your sister again."

She shook her head. "No, Mr. Bingley. Thinking that way will only make things worse. I know my sister. She loved you and would want you to be happy with someone else. So keep your heart open. A year from now, or maybe more, you'll find someone else to love. Someone sweet and kind who will appreciate you."

"Thank you, Miss Eliza."

* * *

The next day, Mr. Darcy requested a meeting with her in his office. They met regularly to discuss Juliette's education, but with the Christmas preparations and Lady Catherine's visit, she had not spoken with him for more than a week. She knocked on his door and he said, "Come in."

He looked up at her, but instead of smiling at her as he usually did, his expression was stern. "What is the problem?" she asked.

"No problem," he said quickly. "At least, I am trying to avoid a problem. Please be seated."

She sat.

"First, I must apologize to you for my mother-in-law's behaviour. I understand that she spoke to you privately yesterday."

Elizabeth bit her lip. "Yes, and I was hoping that she wouldn't relate it all to you. But that was not to be expected."

"No, she is not one to keep her thoughts and feelings to herself. I apologize if she said anything to offend you."

"No. I did not take offense."

"I am glad. I want you to know that I greatly appreciate your work with Juliette and that nothing she said will affect that."

"Thank you."

"However, in the interest of peace for my household, I am going to send you to London for a vacation. Your presence at Pemberley agitates Lady

Catherine."

Her heart sank. "You are dismissing me?"

"No. Absolutely not. I am going to send you to London for a month. You can return after she is gone and Bingley and his sister have left. And the next time we travel to Rosings, you may visit your family as well."

"Will Mrs. Sally go with you to take care of Juliette?"

"Yes. And if you wish, you can write to Juliette. She would appreciate that."

"Yes, sir."

"As soon as you are packed, I will have a carriage and servants ready to accompany you."

"I could take the stage."

"You will not take the stage," he said firmly. "Let me make the arrangements as I see fit."

"Yes, sir."

"If you leave this afternoon, you will be with your family on Christmas Day."

I would rather be with you, she thought, but could not say it. She had made her bed when she refused him and now had to lie in it. "Thank you," she said.

He hesitated as if he wanted to say more, and then added, "I saw you outside with Mr. Bingley yesterday."

She blushed, not knowing what to say. "Yes."

"Perhaps I misunderstood what I saw, and in truth, it is none of my business, but I would still like to know. Is he courting you?"

Elizabeth shook her head. "No. He asked me to marry him, but I turned him down."

Darcy seemed relieved. "You have a habit of declining marriage proposals."

She smiled. 'Yes, my stepmother would not approve."

Again he hesitated and she waited, hoping that he might say more, but then his countenance seemed to change and he said briskly. "That is all. Let Mrs. Reynolds know when you are ready to leave, and I will write to you when it is time for you to return."

"Very good, sir."

"Happy Christmas, Miss Bennet. God bless you on your journey."

She started to say, "Happy Christmas" to him as well, but the well wishes dwindled on her tongue for he had dismissed her and had already turned back to the papers on his desk.

She knew now that Lady Catherine did not need to worry. Mr. Darcy did not love her and he would not be renewing his suit. "Good bye, Mr. Darcy."

CHAPTER FIFTEEN

Christmas in Gracechurch Street was lovely, but Elizabeth found herself out of spirits. She admired the new Gardiner baby—a beautiful chubby girl named Charlotte, met Kitty's fiancé, and went out to the theatre with Mrs. Bennet's beau, a red-faced industrialist from the North named Mr. Hewitt, but her heart was still at Pemberley. When she woke, she wondered what he was doing and what he was feeling. Did she ever cross his mind?

January came and went and February started, with no word from Mr. Darcy. Mrs. Gardiner asked her when she planned to return to Pemberley. "I don't know," she said honestly. "I thought I would have heard by now."

"Perhaps Mr. Darcy has changed his mind," her aunt said kindly. "Why don't you write and tell him that you have decided to stay with us? Kitty will be married in the spring and your mother in the summer. Our house will feel positively empty with only Mary as company. Stay with us, please."

Elizabeth knew that was the logical solution, but she could not accept it. Her heart ached. She wanted to see Mr. Darcy again.

Eventually she got her wish, for in the second week of February; he arrived, requesting an audience with her. When Mrs. Bennet saw his calling card, she said, "Oh, dear. It is that odious Mr. Darcy. I was hoping you had managed to escape, my dear. Well, you tell him that your stepmama is marrying a man that can match his income and you don't need to scrub his floors any longer. You can live with us in Manchester."

Elizabeth said quickly, "Please, mama, lower your voice. He might hear you."

"I don't care if he does."

"And I never scrubbed his floors."

A servant opened the door. "Mr. Darcy," he announced.

When Mr. Darcy came into the room, Elizabeth felt as if her heart would burst. He stood before her, impeccably dressed. His hair was slightly longer than usual and one errant lock fell forward on his forehead. He bowed toward her mother. "Good day, Mrs.

Bennet."

"Mr. Darcy," she said in a tone that was barely civil.

It pained Elizabeth to think that her mother still did not know how much he had done to help her sister Lydia.

"Miss Bennet," he said. "Would you do me the honour of accepting a ride in my curricle? There are a few things I wish to discuss with you privately."

Mrs. Bennet's eyes narrowed. "Indeed?" she said haughtily.

"Mama, he is my employer," Elizabeth reminded her. "And yes, sir. I will get my coat."

"Ask Cook for a hot brick for your feet, my dear," Mrs. Bennet said. "I don't want her to catch cold," she said to Mr. Darcy.

"Neither do I, ma'am. I have extra blankets and will make certain she is kept warm."

"Very well, then," Mrs. Bennet said. "But make certain you are back within an hour, Lizzy, for we have other engagements."

Elizabeth hated to see her stepmother bossing Mr. Darcy, but he took it with good grace. "I will bring her back safely and on time."

Mr. Darcy helped her into the carriage and draped a blanket across her lap. "I am sorry, Miss Bennet. I had hoped to speak to you privately, inside the house, but I realized that with your family that might be impossible."

"I suppose we could have asked to use my uncle's office."

"I did not want to disturb him."

"I agree. A ride is best. It is nice to get outside and enjoy the fresh air."

"I believe you are happiest when you are outside."

She looked at him. I am happiest when I'm with you, she thought. "How soon do you wish me to return to Pemberley? I could be ready today."

Mr. Darcy's lips tightened. "That is what I wished to speak with you about."

Elizabeth's heart filled with dread. "Is there a problem? Is Juliette well?"

"She is fine, and she misses you. But, I have two things to say. First, I no longer wish to employ you as her governess. I have a letter terminating your employment and a letter of recommendation that I will give to you once you are back at home."

Elizabeth gasped. "But why? I thought you were satisfied with my work."

"I am," he said, then said in a frustrated tone. "But I cannot speak to you as I wish when I am driving. Give me a moment and I will find a place to stop."

Elizabeth nodded, too upset to say anything. For a few minutes, he drove down several streets, until he found a place to stop the curricle. He held the reins carefully in one hand and turned to her. "Forgive me, Miss Bennet, I should have handled this better." He gave her the letters.

She did not bother to read them. "If I am no longer your employee, why did you take the effort to come to London to tell me personally? Why did you not write? You said you'd write." Her last few words came out as a sob.

He took her hands in his. "I tried to write to you a hundred times, and I could not do it."

"I don't understand."

"I can see that," he said gently. "Let me explain. When I first offered you a position as Juliette's governess, I promised you that I would never refer to my proposals. As a man of honour, I could not tell you what was in my heart while you were in my employ."

Was he saying what she thought he was saying?

"Every time I tried to write to you, it turned into a love letter."

"Is that why you terminated my employment?"

"Yes, I needed to be able to talk to you freely." He took a deep breath. "And now for the second thing I wished to say. You are too generous to trifle with me. If your feelings are still what they were last April, tell me so at once."

"How could you think that? You know of my regard for you."

"I don't know what to think. My affections and wishes are the same, although they have grown to such an extent that I fear they will overwhelm you. The last few months at Pemberley, I thought perhaps your feelings for me had grown tender, but I could not tell. This is my third and final proposal, Miss Bennet. One word from you will silence me on this subject forever."

Elizabeth's heart beat so rapidly in her chest, she felt almost giddy with relief. He loved her. He still loved her. "I wonder at your courage sir, when I was so unkind twice before."

"No," he said. "Never unkind."

"Then you remember differently than I. But I assume that a reward twice denied increases in its perceived value."

He smiled. "Dearest, loveliest Elizabeth," he said and leaned forward to kiss her.

She knew she ought to stop him, for she had not formally said yes, that she would marry him, but she did not have the strength to refuse him anything.

And then his lips were on hers. It was so different from his Cousin Julian's assault. She sighed and let him kiss her once, then twice. Somehow his arms became wrapped around her and her hands became linked behind his neck. It felt right and comfortable and augured well for a happy marriage. He pulled back so he could look in her eyes.

"What are you thinking?" he asked.

How she loved him. "Odious man," she said, but softened the insult by reaching up to tame that lock of hair that bothered her so. "You nearly caused a fit of apoplexy by giving me that letter. I thought I would never see you again. What would you have done if I had fainted?"

"I would have revived you," he said and kissed her again.

"I think I might like fainting," Elizabeth said, when she could speak, which made him laugh.

The sound filled her with joy. She was amazed that this man, so long out of her reach loved her. She leaned forward to kiss him. "I wish we could go back to Pemberley today."

"So do I. But I agreed to bring you back safe and sound within an hour." He checked the watch on his fob. "So we must return."

Elizabeth winced, remembering Mrs. Bennet's

rudeness. "My stepmother does not like you."

"And my mother-in-law does not like you," he countered. "Somehow we will survive. Since your father is gone, do you think I should speak to Mr. Gardiner?"

"That is a marvellous idea. Thank you."

The next few weeks were busy ones. Mr. Gardiner gave his consent, although as he later told Elizabeth, "It was a mere formality, but I appreciated the gesture."

Mr. Darcy obtained a special license. Rather than marry in London, they chose to marry at the church in Lambton. Most of Elizabeth's family was there, although Lydia and Wickham, blessedly remained in the North. Elizabeth knew that Wickham would never be welcome at Pemberley and she hoped that Lydia would not want to visit by herself. Colonel Fitzwilliam and the Earl of Matlock came as well. Lady Catherine wrote to say that she was too ill to come to the wedding but that she expected to see them both at Rosings at Easter.

"That is her way of chastising or punishing us for marrying and yet offering an olive branch," Darcy said. "You do not need to go in the spring, if you don't wish to."

"No, I don't mind Lady Catherine. Not as long as

I have you."

Juliette was thrilled to learn that her beloved Miss Bennet would soon become Mrs. Darcy. "May I call you Mama?" she asked.

Elizabeth hugged her. "Of course, darling."

During the ceremony, Mrs. Bennet cried and Elizabeth thought fondly of her father. She thought he would be amused to think that she had fallen in love with Mr. Darcy. She thought they would have liked each other, if they had been given the chance. Mr. Gardiner stood in her father's place to give her away.

She also thought of Jane, who had correctly guessed that although she was frustrated and annoyed by Mr. Darcy at Netherfield, she had liked him just a little. Jane would be happy for her.

Mr. Bingley came alone to the wedding. Miss Bingley could not attend for she was busy preparing for the Season. At the wedding breakfast at Pemberley, he wished them both well and said to Elizabeth, "I should have noticed earlier that you were made for each other. I am sorry I was oblivious. I hope my prior sentiments in December did not cause you any unrest."

"None at all," Elizabeth said.

"Speak for yourself," Darcy said and laughed. "I

was a green-eyed monster."

Elizabeth looked at him thoughtfully. "Truly?"

He nodded.

"Then you hid it well."

"I have many hidden depths that I wish to share with you."

Elizabeth blushed. Her aunt had spoken to her several days before about the marriage bed. Elizabeth was looking forward to becoming one with her husband, but she still had a little apprehension.

Rather than go away for a honeymoon, they planned to stay at Pemberley and take a trip later in the summer. The wedding day was long, but eventually the guests left and the household was quiet. Elizabeth dismissed her lady's maid and waited for her husband.

He knocked on the door.

"Come in," she said quietly.

As he walked into the room, her breath caught. He was such a tall, handsome man. She remembered how impressed she had been when she first saw him at the Meryton Ball. And now he was her husband. He held open his arms and she walked into them. "Ah, Elizabeth," he said, holding her close. "How long I have waited for this day."

She breathed in the warm masculine scent of him.

She could not resist teasing him. "Am I more than tolerable now? Handsome enough to tempt you?"

He groaned. "I regret those words, and they proved to be completely false. For I have never been so tempted by a woman in my life."

He kissed her long and deep until she sighed against him. "I am glad."

Much later when the candles were gutted and her new husband was asleep beside her, Elizabeth contemplated the day. There was much to think on. Her husband had been tender and gentle and yet had thrilled her as well. The physical intimacies of marriage were surprising and new to her, but she sensed that they would grow even better with time.

She rested her head on his broad chest. He stirred and drew her closer with his arm. She sighed, loving the feel of him, his comforting solid presence. She knew she could trust him. He would care for her and respect her. She would no longer be alone. He would be her ally and confidante.

She had thought for months that Pemberley had become her home, but now in the quiet of her wedding night, she realized that Fitzwilliam Darcy was her home.

EPILOGUE

"Fitzwilliam. Darling. It is time." His wife's words brought him out of a deep sleep and made him sit up in bed.

"Are you certain?" He saw that she had already lit a candle by the side of the bed.

She smiled at his befuddlement. "Yes, this is my third time. I am certain. In truth, I have been lying here for several hours, feeling the birthing pains, but now I think it is time to send for Mrs. Ostley."

"You should have woken me earlier."

"No," she said calmly. "You needed your sleep. I did not want to kick you out of bed any earlier than necessary."

Unlike many couples of their generation, he and Elizabeth shared the same bed. He kept his own room for the sake of appearances, but he rarely slept there.

He rang a bell for a servant and sent word for the

midwife to join them. "And I will get dressed," he said to Elizabeth.

"Yes, although you have very handsome dressing gown, I would prefer it to be for my view only," she said, then winced as her body contracted.

"Minx," he said, and kissed her.

He thought he had loved her when they first married eight years before, but since then his love had grown even greater. She was a continual delight: a true companion – his mental and physical equal. Not only did she challenge him intellectually, she matched him passion for passion. He knew he was a blessed man.

Once her lady's maid appeared, he stepped through the adjoining door to his bedroom. There, he dressed quickly and quietly.

He knew he should not be so worried. Elizabeth was strong and healthy and had already given birth to two beautiful sons. This third pregnancy had progressed equally well with no signs of trouble. But there were always risks with childbirth. Elizabeth never seemed to worry, which surprised him since her mother had died in childbirth, and he tried to keep his fears to himself.

As a parent, she was the more adventurous one, often encouraging their children to take risks, whereas he was the more cautious one, teaching them about dangers and consequences. He felt that their natural tendencies worked well together, balancing each other.

Juliette was a young woman now, almost fourteen. She was natural athlete. She enjoyed swimming and running, and was an excellent horsewoman. She spent hours in the stables. Darcy worried that she might not marry, but Elizabeth told him not to be ridiculous. "The heiress of Rosings will have no difficulty finding a husband," she assured him. "Somewhere out there is an excellent man who will love her just the way she is. Just as there was someone for me."

He had rewarded that sentiment with a kiss.

The boys, Thomas and John, were seven and five. Thomas, the heir to Pemberley, was bookish and had a talent for mathematics. John had not learned to read yet, but had a calm, steady temper and a keen eye for detail. Elizabeth thought he might become a scientist.

Darcy was so glad he had married Elizabeth, for not only had she provided him with more children, she had helped him become a better father. She had taught him to laugh and to savour life's pleasures. Sometimes he still got caught up in his many duties as Master of Pemberley, but then she would lovingly draw him out. Surprisingly, he had even learned to enjoy dancing.

When he returned to Elizabeth's bedroom, he saw that the sheets had been replaced with fresh ones and Elizabeth was wearing one of his nightshirts rather than one of her gowns. He raised his eyebrows but said nothing. He had learned early on in their marriage that she could be unconventional. She saw his surprise and smiled. "My gowns are all too long for birthing. I thought your shirt would be more convenient and much more comfortable."

"Whatever makes you happy," he said, watching with amusement as she rolled up the sleeves on his shirt to bare her arms.

"And I've asked Georgiana to sit with me."

Within a few minutes, Georgiana joined them. She was Mrs. Bingley now, and lived with Charles in a neighbouring county, only thirty miles away. She had been visiting for a week.

For the first few years after their marriage, he and Elizabeth had thought Charles would never marry. But then one summer, when Georgiana was twenty, he came to visit, and what had been a steady friendship between them had blossomed into love. Elizabeth had been pleased. "I think Jane would approve."

Darcy stayed as long as he could, until the midwife ordered him out of the room. After that, he paced and went to Pemberley's chapel to say a prayer.

When the boys woke, he ate breakfast with them. He then roamed the halls, trying to read, trying not to hear the alarming sounds from his bedchamber. But eventually a servant came to fetch him.

"Is Mrs. Darcy well?" he asked.

"Yes, sir."

He ran up to the bedroom. Elizabeth was lying in bed, with her hair neatly combed and a fresh lace cap on her head. He saw that she was no longer in his nightshirt and was now wearing a nightgown. In her arms was a beautiful baby wrapped in a blanket. He sat down on the side of the bed, being careful not to jostle her. "What did we get this time?" he asked. "Another boy?"

"No, a girl."

He beamed at her and kissed her. "Excellent, Mrs. Darcy."

"I am thinking of naming her Anne," she said.

His heart was touched. As a second wife, she had always been respectful of his first. As she had told him once, "If it were not for Anne de Bourgh, there would have been no Juliette, and I never would have become her governess. And then I would never have fallen in love with you and never married you."

He liked to think that somehow they would have found each other, even if he had not been married and widowed first, but that was a question of fate for the philosophers. He said, "Don't you want to name her Jane?"

She smiled. "I'll save that name for our next daughter."

"How many children are you planning to have?"

"As many as you'll give me, Mr. Darcy."

There was a gleam in her eye that warmed his heart. He thought back to the day years before when he had decided it was his duty to marry again. He had thought he had known what he wanted, and yet he had found much so more in Elizabeth. "That will be my pleasure, Mrs. Darcy."

The End

AUTHOR'S NOTE:

I hope you enjoyed *Master of Pemberley*. I still feel a little guilty killing off Jane, so I'm not sure I'll do that again.

One thing I enjoy about writing Pride and Prejudice Variations is creating the side characters. We don't really know much about Anne de Bourgh or Colonel Fitzwilliam from the original novel. So they can be completely different people in each of my variations.

And of course, there can be a thousand different versions of Darcy.

You may enjoy one of my other stories, *Darcy Unmasked*. In it, the ball at Netherfield is a masquerade, which changes everything.

To find out about my other Darcy stories, you can go to my website http://www.janegrix.com.

For those of you that are interested, I also write

sweet quirky romances under the name Beverly Farr.

Happy reading,
Jane

And now, for a bonus, an excerpt from *Not Romantic* by L. K. Rigel. This book made me laugh out loud and I liked reading about Charlotte Lucas, even if she wasn't romantic.

From:
Not Romantic: A Pride and Prejudice Variation
Copyright 2015 L.K. Rigel
Published by Beastie Press

Chapter 3 ~ Mercenaries
Lucas Lodge

Charlotte

ALL WAS LOST! Charlotte had tried for Mr. Collins enthusiastically, at times almost recklessly, but her endeavors had gone unrewarded. He was to return to Hunsford this very day, empty-handed—no engagement at all having been secured by anybody.

Charlotte sat at the desk in her bedroom and gazed out the window. There were no clouds this morning in late November, but a brisk wind whipped through the nearest trees and the tall shrubs along the lane. She looked down at the list of tasks and errands which she was composing. With each item, she felt herself fall back into her daily routine.

She wanted to cry.

She had believed he was hers. After the *infamous rejection*, as Lydia called it, Mr. Collins had come to Lucas Lodge for lunch, stayed past dinner, and only with great reluctance had returned to Longbourn. He had taken to walking in the morning after breakfast, and his walks had brought him nearly every day to her door.

It had been wonderful! Her parents had both

dropped the pitiful cast to their expressions when speaking to her. Lady Lucas had summoned Mrs. Dawson and ordered a new pelisse for Charlotte and had made her a present of a favorite silk fan. For the first time in years, Charlotte felt she had the means to be a credit to her family and not a burden.

But he had not offered.

Perhaps she should feel guilty for pursuing Longbourn's heir… but she did not! Eliza had rejected him. Incomprehensible. As no one else seemed to want him, Charlotte had done every practical thing to secure the gentleman's attentions to herself.

She'd applied the very advice she'd freely given regarding Jane and Mr. Bingley, attempting to secure Mr. Collins with all haste. The advice had elicited Eliza's smiles when given. Charlotte shuddered to think what humor her friend would find in it now.

She would allow she had acted in a manner most mercenary. But she would not feel guilty.

A door in the hall opened, and Lady Lucas's gentle voice sounded in the corridor. With a twinge of irritation, Charlotte realized that when she had come up from breakfast she'd left her bedroom door ajar. Sure enough, it was nine thirty, the time Mama generally emerged from her own room.

How lovely it must be to breakfast leisurely in one's room! To gently ease into the day's activity. When Charlotte was twenty-three, she had one morning told her maid to bring her breakfast up to her room, thinking to establish the practice as her own. She was a grown woman, after all!

But that pleasure belonged only to married ladies. Lady Lucas had made as much clear when she put a quick end to what she called naught but an indulgence in an unmarried lady. Charlotte had felt humiliated at the time, embarrassed for having assumed an unearned privilege.

In the interests of household peace, she accepted her mama's chastisement, but she had gone without breakfast that morning as her own secret demonstration of resentment. Neither she nor Lady Lucas had ever spoken of the incident again.

She sighed absently and rose to go close her door.

"Mama!" The happy shout accompanied the sound of Gwendolyn scampering through the hallway. Every morning, she waited for their mother in the window seat at the end of the upstairs hall. Charlotte paused with her ear to her door.

"Good morning, dearest," Lady Lucas said.

"Good morning, Mama."

The footsteps of mother and daughter click-clacked lightly against the wood floor, then went silent as they reached the bolted carpet runner on the stairs. Charlotte's father was not a wealthy man, but he did aspire to do credit to that gentility which his title, acquired in midlife, demanded. From time to time, an improvement to the beauty or comfort of Lucas Lodge would appear, the latest being Turkey carpet runners on all but the servants' staircases.

Again Charlotte sighed. She was like a bird in a pleasant cage. Quite pleasant. How dare she complain? Her father was geniality itself. And though her mother always looked at her with faint disappointment, she had never given Charlotte an unkind word.

And yet...

And yet, if Charlotte did not escape this place, she would go mad. She did not know how much longer she could endure her mother's ill-concealed disappointment, her father's purposeful good cheer, Maria's pity, or her brother's barely-disguised dread at the prospect of supporting her when their father should no longer be with them.

If she were honest with herself, she'd admit that nothing could have stopped her from putting herself in Mr. Collins's way. These past few days, they *all* had nurtured high hopes of him.

But what did it matter? Her attentions, subtle or not, to the young rector—for he was two years her junior—had come to naught. In one or two instances, she had thought him about to request a private interview, but either his courage had failed or she had misread his expression. Now it was too late. Indeed, he may have already left Hertfordshire.

She returned to the desk at her window, filled her pen, and began to write.

All is…

Movement drew her attention to the world outside. At the end of the lane, something large and dark charged along near the giant rhododendron. Charlotte caught her breath and leaped to her feet. Where had she put her shawl?

It was too early in the morning to call—and Mr. Collins had often said that he was an ardent admirer of the proper forms—yet there he was, and here he came, striding purposively, hand on his hat to protect it against the wind. He stopped in the lane, his lips moving as though he were practicing a speech.

Not daring a smile, Charlotte bent over and finished writing the sentence she'd begun—with a different, and opposite, meaning:

…NOT lost!

~*~

William

William Collins knew his worth, even if *some people* did not!

The morning was crisp and cold, and he gratefully drew biting air deep into his lungs. Once or twice a gust of wind made it necessary to grab onto his hat; otherwise, his tumultuous thoughts commanded the majority of his attention.

There was his painful visit to Longbourn—near its end, thank Providence, and best forgotten. He had not expected or deserved the treatment given him at his future estate. It was not his fault he was the heir to that amiable house and its lands. *Amiable.* Well, yes. Until the young ladies of Longbourn opened their mouths. What cacophony! And their mother! How a woman could alternate with such rapidity from ingratiating to shrill and back again he would never know.

But it were best to leave that subject alone.

He'd come to Hertfordshire with the intention to offer marriage to any Bennet daughter who would prove likely, for Longbourn was entailed to a male descendent—himself—and they were all of them, most assuredly, female. He could not save them all from the poverty and obscurity which must certainly await their futures, but was it not praiseworthy that he was willing to ensure one a place as the future mistress of Longbourn?

After all, in advising that it was time he marry, Lady Catherine had never said *explicitly* that he should marry one of the Bennet girls. She'd approved of the suggestion, but she wasn't *invested* in it, as well she might had the idea been her own.

No. It had been his aim to act in an honorable and thoughtful manner. Did they not all understand that, having married one Bennet daughter, he would be obligated to see that none was ever without a home or shunted off to be a governess or hat maker?

No. They had laughed at him—especially *that Lydia*—and whispered behind his back. *That Kitty* had looked ill at the thought of being his Mrs. Collins. Even lovely and serene Jane had lost her composure a little when the subject arose.

And Miss Elizabeth Bennet…

Cousin Elizabeth and her father were two peas in a pod. After all the effort he'd taken to supply many little elegant compliments as could be adapted to them—and which he had practiced so as to make them with as unstudied an air as possible!—he was certain both Miss Elizabeth and Mr. Bennet had smirked at him behind their fans, in a manner of speaking.

Of the five Bennet daughters, only Cousin Mary had appeared somewhat unappalled at the prospect of becoming his wife. Indeed, the thought of the middle Bennet daughter had flitted across his brain that morning as he'd waited for her sister.

If Elizabeth will not—the words had actually popped into his mind—*Mary most likely will.*

But the idea of Mary—the idea of *any* Bennet daughter—had been rendered repugnant to him by the end of Elizabeth's most eloquent and ardent rejection. Quite frankly, her fervor had unseated his confidence. He'd been momentarily adrift, shaken, his certainty that any one of them would be thrilled to receive his proposal… destroyed.

It shattered all notions of common sense. In what else about the world had he been so utterly mistaken?

The mother had understood at once the ramifications of Elizabeth's foolishness, and the fervor of her attempt to reverse the error had stabilized his moorings. But then the father had rallied to his daughter's cause and had ensured the damage was irreparable.

The wound inflicted in that hour was healing, and more quickly than he'd imagined possible. William felt sorry for the girls, that they had such a… well, he hated to even think it, but there it was:

Mr. Bennet was careless as to his daughters' interests. Even reckless, one might say. What had he ever done for his family... except try to get them a brother?

William, stop! It is un-Christian and unworthy of you to make even a silent witticism regarding such a sad, sad subject.

He did not know what would happen to the Bennet girls, but his duty toward them had been met. He had tried to secure their welfare. He'd been rejected. There was an end on it. Before two more hours passed, he would leave Longbourn.

His chief preoccupation at the moment was with what lay before him in that brief time. On the now-familiar lane from Longbourn to Lucas Lodge, each step away from one toward the other calmed him. Images of Bennets receded from his mind.

Miss Lucas, on the other hand...

Ah. Miss Charlotte Lucas was an entirely different matter. Such serenity. Such poise. Such kindness in both tone and intention! He hoped—oh, dare he hope?—that she would not find him ridiculous. He was well aware that he *was* ridiculous in this: no gentleman who wasn't an Italian should fall in love three times (for he must admit Miss Jane Bennet had briefly excited his heartstrings) in one fortnight.

He must hope that Charlotte would believe he had come to love and esteem her above all women. This had the virtue of being true, but he was no longer confident of truth's effectiveness in matters of the heart.

Thank Providence for Charlotte. Miss Charlotte Lucas, Elizabeth Bennet's good friend. An involuntary smile twitched at William's lips, and he felt his features soften. He noticed a spot of sunshine that made the dew glitter at his feet, and the happy song of morning birds in a yew tree nearby.

Amiable Charlotte—in his thoughts he dared call her by her Christian name. Charlotte had taken pity on him, guided him away from shattered equanimity into the genial comfort which marked her sphere of influence. When she looked into his eyes, he felt understood. And he realized now that he'd noticed this before, at the card party at Lucas Lodge and the ball at Netherfield. Whenever she was near, he felt it impossible that he should falter in… in whatever he might have a mind to attempt.

The daughter of a knight, Sir William Lucas. Didn't *that* sound well! Lady Catherine could not object to that.

Indeed, it was quite likely that his patroness would

prefer the alternative outcome he now hoped to bring about. Yes. Lady Catherine would much prefer to see him married to the daughter of a knight than of a country gentleman who could not even provide a dowry.

And Longbourn… Longbourn would be his at all events.

_*_

Charlotte

Charlotte flew down the stairs, throwing her shawl about her shoulders. She remembered her bonnet only because it was in her path, hanging on the stand in the foyer. She raced outside to the lane and had barely finished tying the ribbons under her chin when he came round the giant holly at the edge of the front garden.

He was a large man, more awkward than commanding. He was not witty or clever; Charlotte knew with certainty that Eliza would think her a fool to accept such a fool. His gaze stumbled over her, and the light of recognition followed. All his attention seized upon her, and she suddenly felt the weight of the reality of what—until this moment—had been mere daydream.

Their eyes met, each aware of the question in the air between them.

There might have been a moment when she could have turned it all back. Could have put on the mantle of civility, frozen him in the ice of polite manners, and refused to understand him.

But Charlotte's good sense took the reins. With determination more than joy, she smiled and nodded her encouragement to Mr. Collins, and each knew what her answer to his question would be.

~*~

*Vist www.lkrigel.com/accomplished-ladies/
to learn more about **Not Romantic***

Made in the USA
Charleston, SC
23 July 2016